L. H. Westerlund is a Scandinavian author, engineer and classic literature enthusiast living in London. She is currently working on several new novels, including a sequel for the *University Strange Series*.

To my grandfather Ernst Elfton for being my Arador.
I love you and I miss you.

L. H. Westerlund

University Strange or My Life Amongst Academics

Austin Macauley Publishers™

LONDON • CAMBRIDGE • NEW YORK • SHARJAH

A CIP catalogue record for this title is available from the British Library.

ISBN 9781788484176 (Paperback)
ISBN 9781528956703 (ePub e-book)

www.austinmacauley.com

First Published (2019)
Austin Macauley Publishers Ltd
25 Canada Square
Canary Wharf
London
E14 5LQ

Thank you twenty-three times to my mother, Ida, for always being my most honest and supportive critic. I love you, and it means so much to me that you believe in me.

Table of Contents

Chapter 1

Sigh. I closed yet another absolutely abysmal vampire novel about a special and powerful heroine, possessing powers out of the scale; a strong, proud woman, who still was only yet another horny teenager. Did every modern heroine have to be only lustful? Was there no other conflict in the entire known universe worth pursuing writing about?

"You know, for a person who hates books, you read quite a lot." I looked up, mostly for politeness sake rather than out of curiosity. The voice was unmistakable. Just like myself, my best friend was unimpressed by books, and unlike me, he rarely read them, but my current visitor did not share in this distrust.

Dhrar looked at me with a mischievous smile so typical for the tall, athletic Djinn. Hir gave me a headshake and suggested that I might try to read something which didn't suck. Dhrar might have been a walking, talking mystery, granted, but a fucking *smart* walking, talking mystery.

Most people might not know, but some would actually be able to tell you, to some extent and with slight variations, what a Djinn is. The word 'hir' though, wasn't anything your *typical* mortal would know. Because of the sexless, or maybe androgynous—I do not have any freaking idea—nature of the Djinn, we had made a middle word for them, inspired by the name they already bore. Well, the angels did. They are the undisputed masters of getting their noses where they do not in any way belong, after all.

This was immediately proven, with the help of the appearance of my best friend, Alexis Darn. He was dark beyond example, or at least he appeared that way, and his wings were white as snow. Or, the feathers he occasionally could be persuaded to give to my brother, the scientist, upon losing them, were white. Alexis had, a ridiculous number of years ago, cut his own wings off for some mythical reason he always hid behind the utter bullshit of 'wanting to fit into the world of men'. It wasn't just inane, it *wasn't* even imaginative. Or even the least bit logical, if you knew Alex even a little, which I suppose practically nobody did, which might have been why it worked in the first place.

"Now what?" he wondered, accidentally strengthening my, yet never, gainsaid theory that angels could never mind their own business. All right, he was my friend, but still. Always curious. Just as singularly empathic and loyal, oh *yes*, but *whatever*.

"All books I read are just full of excuses for cool heroines to get less cool by falling a hundred miles for the wrong guy and spend the entire book wondering if they will soon lose their virginity," I complained. "And I am not even counting this last one. She isn't just pathetic and yearning, she is so utterly *useless*!"

"Well, that'll match her up nicely with him then," the Djinn noted with a shrug and threw hirself down onto a sofa that wasn't actually there. "I've never known anyone that grumpy for no good reason. Or for any reason."

"He is her teacher, though," I noted rather vaguely. "He could be right to be pessimistic, judging by the statistics." Alex gave us a rather blank look, only to apparently—rather despondently—reach the conclusion that we hadn't actually lost our sanity this time either. I could easily figure that he found us to be fairly near the edge, so to speak. Not that he would have actually minded if we had lost it, to be perfectly frank.

"We all have to get to be lustful sometimes, it's a part of life!" we were assured by a hastily appearing djinn named Robin, who I always thought of as female, for some reason. "Even us!"

"I am not the slightest bit full of flight..." Dhrar objected neutrally, and, judging by the words, fairly absent-mindedly, too. Hir then gave a grin, "Unless you're discussing the Lamborghini Gallardo Balboni, *oh dear* what a car!"

Robin and I gave simultaneous moans, but not at all for the same reasons. Hir gave a resigned groan, I was equally as in love with the car as Dhrar was. I'm telling you, Rob is a girl. Which I am too, fine, but who says that that has to matter. It isn't as if most guys are more focused on the cars than the girls they could score in one, anyway.

And if I ever want a date, I will go find Thomas. The dude is a perfect matchmaker, complete lack of people skills aside, if he only would get the idea into his head to try, what with his ability to 'sense' all and everybody. He would find me a good match straight away. I wouldn't be the first to come to him from crush related circumstances, either, but hardly for that very reason.

Apparently, he is attractive; or so they say. And I am sure they're right, but as it happens, he is my annoying, kind and on top of that, *wise* big brother. The only thing even REMOTELY close to how much I hate that git is how much I love him. But don't tell him that. He is nine years my elder and was twenty the year our mum left and our dad was burnt alive in our house. Which he set on fire himself to get rid of her. Oh, the irony.

Since nobody was thinking of me at this instance, but merely tried their best to off one another any way that they could, it came down to the science nerd and (probably not) involuntary heartbreaker Thomas to pick up the pieces, namely myself. I moved into the University Strange (no, that is not the formal name, sadly) and watched in growing boredom how he expanded the known boundaries of knowledge and science with his exceedingly dull experiments.

Finally, someone had the bright idea that I might be of some use and designated me the job to monitor the suicide attempts of a scientist, Stanley. Which might not have been an entirely appropriate task for a child, not to mention not such a terrible waste of time, had the man actually been in the least suicidal, which he truly never was. Stanley *loves* life, slightly too much for his own good, actually, and him spending his days and years at a university isn't a floop, either. He is a scientist with all his heart, and he truly *loves* his work. The resulting consequence is that he lives and learns with great enthusiasm and *that* resulting consequence is completely freaking life threatening. The dude never has the least idea what he's doing. *Ever*.

At long last, I turned my attention back towards my mates. Robin was sitting in the sofa that still wasn't there, cosily curled up besides Dhrar while they discussed something in djinn. Alexis stood a ways away, absentmindedly scratching his back, while a few white downs fell out from underneath his black shirt and onto the floor. And I was still sitting on the only chair in my office, with a boring book in my lap and my computer blinking for some reason known only onto to itself next to me.

"How are you doing that?" the question that I had asked for near enough every day for literally years now had both djinns smiling.

"Well," Robin leaned back nonchalantly.

"Pure awesome talent," Dhrar added. "We are so terribly talented." Alexis tossed something that looked kind of (or rather exactly) like a fistful of air in their direction and they both fell into the floor with a crash.

"Hardly," the angel got the last word, looking completely unfazed. Both the djinns, who were angrier than they would admit that he had spoiled their magic, threw something back. Water or perhaps ice for Dhrar and fire for Robin. Alexis wasn't even looking. A casual gesture performed with *one finger* stopped all attempts at magic. Only when the djinns turned vaguely green I realised what he'd done. He had stolen their magic fully.

Since I was the only one that could, I tossed my perfectly terrible book at him. He dodged it easily enough, but it somewhat ruffled his always equally neglected hair. "You are not allowed to do that," I snapped at him.

He kindly, in his usual neutral way, looked back at me. "Their magic isn't like your legs," he informed me melodically, "it will grow back."

"I know that, but it is equally important!" I objected, letting all the rage I had promised myself not to take out on them merely for appearing, right out. "Just because you're capable of doing anything you'd like it doesn't mean you have the right to!"

Alexis, insightful and, to me, anyway, endlessly patient, simply came over to hug me. "Easy," he comforted me simply, naturally knowing that I was in pain, and the dual reasons why. The pain in my right wrist because of my fall the day before, and the other pain, which I would actually place in the small of the back, if I had to give it a space, because of things I myself thought I really should have gotten over by now. Almost seven years had passed since my parents died, dammit, but that apparently didn't help.

Even aside from the spooky ability to read thoughts, which I knew Alexis possessed, but neither needed at the moment nor would ever use on me, he knew, of course he knew, what made me rest my head against his chest and want to accept the comfort he was offering.

"You were actually there when they had that duel," had been his response when I had once asked him if he didn't think it was weird that I still got upset about that sometimes, "and you were old enough to remember it, clearly. I can imagine fairly few things *less* strange."

Alexis looked at me, and his… fire-blue eyes, to use my own expression, which if I may say so myself is the best one, visibly grew darker before me until they were so dark blue that the colour only glimmered in the black. "Do you want me to remove the pain for you?" he asked for my permission. I was the only one he ever asked for permission before uttering a spell. To be frank, he scared the shit out of most of the university residents, and for good reason.

I actually flinched. Removing the pain I felt about my parents was something he had never suggested before, and it would mean a very intrusive magic; to change me inside to remove something which had left an effect on my soul, for lack of a better term. Surprisingly enough, Alex laughed at my dismay. Sure, he often laughed at the effect he had on people, but he never laughed at me.

"No, no," he ensured me with an unusual crooked smile (him smiling wasn't unusual in itself, but that was a new look). "Not that pain—I'd like to help you with your hand!" I broke down into a complete giggle attack and offered him my arm. Holy cricket. How stupid could you get? Even if you read teenage literature? I mean, they say you are what you read (which I don't believe) but surely that is stretching it?

Of course, Alexis wouldn't risk that. He out of anyone wouldn't risk changing me in any way. It was likely it wasn't even *possible*—considering the advanced tattoo, filled to the brim with every protective spell he had been able to think of, placed underneath my right collarbone and which gamely formed whatever motive I fancied if I only touched it and wished. That last part was pretty needless, as it was a half broken feather. It was always a feather.

When I was younger, I had asked it to make a swan, a paw, butterflies and a tree, but I had always returned to the feather, and now I had since long stopped trying. It was a goddamned feather, and *sod it*.

I sat down, without an ounce of surprise, secure in the comfortable, and enormous, blue armchair which Alex had made to magically appear in the middle of the room, and let him sit down on the armrest to check my wrist. The djinns were watching us as if it was a show of some kind, but it was, of course. Alexis was one of the most powerful magicians in the world, the undisputedly tenfold best at the entire university (and the place was pretty well stocked on the advanced, not to say *awesome*) and now they got to see him expertly practicing a magic that nobody could get him to touch normally.

While Alexis rolled up the sleeve of my tunic and started to check the damage to be able to choose a spell, I turned back to the djinns. Dhrar, who was a very typical Djinn who cared a lot for tradition, looked very lost without hir magic. I felt sorry for hir. Alexis might be my closest friend, but I had known Dhrar since I first started studying, and we had kept each other company studying a thousand times. Alexis was never quite able to understand problems with difficult homework or studies, but Dhrar could. Alexis was always happy to help me out, but had he ever decided to enter the lesson system, he would have been obliged to tutor our teachers. Dhrar and I were equals, if that can ever be said about magical creatures and human beings.

Robin, who was more of a modernist Djinn, I had known for about two years now. Hir was sitting by the wall, giving us murderous looks. I frowned. I was the first to admit, hir had a pretty good reason to be pissed off at Alex at this point, but hir *seemed* to look at us both. I shrugged that thought off and instead pointed out, "But Robin, you cut your hair off!" The Djinn smiled. Robin had used to have hir dark hair long, but it was now as short as the classical Djinn style worn by Dhrar. Angels usually had long hair and Djinns short, for some reason, and humans couldn't make their mind up which.

"Do you like it?" Robin wondered with a smile, "classical me!" I nodded my head, but Dhrar gave hir an almost suspicious look.

"You are usually all about the human culture," hir objected, "why are you suddenly taking distance from it? It isn't that it isn't nice, it's just so very unlike you." Hir added quickly.

"You have to try some new things!" Robin answered with a shrug, just as I expected form hir. That was classic Robin behaviour, and not djinnish in the least.

At that same moment, Alexis said simply, "All right, sparrow, I will start healing now."

About seven seconds had passed, approximately, when he sighed and muttered, "Incompetent idiots." I looked up at him, without bothering to pronounce the question out loud, and he explained gamely, despite his sudden grumpiness. "They have started the healing process for you and eased the pain, briefly, but seriously. Why should you carry this around?"

"Too much healing magic will harm the one it is performed on, uses up their own power," I reminded him.

17

"Yes, but it is also about the skill of the magician. This is only one small broken bone, *what* kind of novices are they really?" he had now reached the exploding point of his temper. Outrage or no outrage, his grip around my wrist didn't grow even remotely tighter. The anger wasn't for me.

The Djinns had curled up, where they sat on the floor, leaning against the wall, and I understood them. Unless I deterred him, someone or *someones* were likely to very soon lose their lives, or at least something else that they would much rather keep, and dearly miss.

"They can hardly help that they aren't you. There are quite *a few* magicians and quite *few* you," I reminded him sternly. Dhrar and Robin didn't understand how I had the nerve, but what was he going to do? We were friends, truly, friends, and he would never ever raise a hand at me. So why shouldn't I yell at him? Especially as I was the only one with these privileges and somebody *needed* to yell at him, regularly.

To the surprise of our now somewhat expanded audience, but never mine, Alexis merely smiled, as the darkness of his eyes gave forewarning of truly awesome magic approaching quickly. "All right, all right," he surrendered readily. "May I heal you now, please?" At this point, there was quite a few people standing in the doorway, or sneaking by the wall to join the Djinns, to watch Alexis heal. Obviously, they did not escape his attention.

"Are they bothering you?" he merely asked me. I knew they would be evicted very quickly if I said that they did, but having grown up amongst academics, I knew very well that more than anything, they liked to observe occurrences, were it science or magic, that were out of the norm. For me, indulging them was mostly a given. However, I spotted Kata, whom I did not like at all, hiding in a corner.

"Of course not," I smiled. "Do you realise the shame if I let the great Alexis *heal* without including Dhrar? Thor, no!" Alexis merely laughed and waited for the continuation he knew would come.

"But," I gave a short nod in Kata's general direction, "do I even need to explain myself?" Alexis promptly turned her upside down, which completely messed up her hair but did not achieve anything else as her clothes were so tight, sent her fairly softly into the ceiling and then dropped her to about an inch above the ground where he let her slide off all the way to the stairs, which she fell down with a revealing rattle. I did not need to ask to know that she didn't get hurt. Alexis was well aware that I preferred my conflicts solved a little less violently than he could sometimes do.

Alexis then turned his attention to my arm, and after a glance at me did something which really made me feel warm and appreciated inside. He showcased his gift, rightly said a small piece of it, letting everyone see the colours of magic he used. This was normal to almost all magicians, at least as soon as formulas or spells turned the least bit tough, but Alexis's magic was always completely undiscoverable. Only the most skilled masters could even feel it, and we were no longer talking about petty spells if it came to that. They had to look pretty thoroughly, and he had to really work hard. I doubted that even this masterful healing would leave any trace.

But now he readily showed all the magic he used. The magicians in the room, no doubt drawn here by a spell from someone close by, could read it all out with ease. Alexis did not enjoy giving into weakness or show off what he did; but this he let everyone see. He did it for me, because I wanted him to, and the feeling of friends like that is to die for. No matter if they are almost all-powerful magicians, or simply your friends.

Not even thirty, if even twenty, seconds had passed, when he cursed and his magic turned black in rage. "What idiot was it really that helped you?" he hissed, voice full of anger which obviously was turned on anyone but me, never mind the fact that I was the one he spoke to.

"One of the healers," I answered patiently. I could see from the corner of my eye how pale the sister of the man who had healed me had become.

"He has wrought your hand inside out, no wonder that you've been in pain!" Alexis raged on. The call of science, or magic, in all honour, most left us at this point. They were well aware by now that I needed neither help nor protection, but were aware that did they stay, they might. Only a couple of real nerds remained behind.

"Now, don't do anything stupid," I warned Alex and then turned to them. "I would like some privacy now," I enlightened them. Half of them were liable to never have listened to me in any normal case, not about anything this important and interesting, anyway, but Alex was perched on the armrest of my chair and was gathering up air in the palm of his hand. There was no need for him to even threaten them. "Give them ten seconds to leave," I suggested as one of them tripped over another in urgency to obey.

"All right," had he been the arch villain in a movie, or, what do I know, maybe real life as well, he would have given me a diabolical smile. Truth is that his neutral expression was worse by far. "Ten seconds." If only evacuations in case of fire had been that effective.

When the scientists had disappeared, I looked around the room. It was a fairly large, empty room with light walls and dark oak floors. A red desk chair of IKEA's armchair type was set before a very small, dark desk containing only a laptop, turned on and blinking vaguely, as well as dust in the corners.

Some people, the ones that didn't see my grades, to be precise, came to the natural conclusion that my work room looked like it did because I wasn't very interested in studies. The truth was that it looked like it did because I wasn't a *complete* and *utter idiot*. The desk was indeed that small because there was no need to fit books upon it, but this did not mean that I never *read* books.

Why on earth would I study in a *completely* uninspiring room surrounded by rooms containing more clueless students and the odd teacher, tired out of their mind of life and stupid students? Almost every friend I had was a djinn, which practically meant that they were shells, full to the brim of the pure magic that set their entire kind aside from all other beings.

The two men I called my family, practically the only family I had; my brother and my best friend, were simply the most distinguished within their respective fields. Though to be fair, Alexis was either amongst the first, or the *actual* first, within *every* field.

So why would I study alone, when I could study under their guidance? My brother's 'library',—which was by far the most fitting description of his mysterious mix of a workshop and a living room—was the type of place where there were always too many books, but which yet always had space for a few more. So I could easily sprawl out on his huge, thick carpet, that covered half the floor between the book cases, spread my books around me and learn anything in far more peace than I could find at the students' corridor at any time. Much better.

In Alexis' even larger, elegant, impressive and super magical workshop (to mention only a few suitable adjectives) stood an impressive oak desk which very well accommodated every book I had ever owned, probably at the same time, and Alexis, who always worked standing up, had long announced it was too low for him to work at.

That last part was so very obviously obfuscating, not to mention an outright lie, for so many reasons, but I was not in the habit of forcing him to show me any obvious warmth if he'd rather not. If he wanted to be aloof, I let him. But fact is that it was mine, and I spent most of my study time sitting at it.

Alex could spend hours explaining reasoning to me that at least the first few years probably was so basic to him that it could be compared to asking me to hold a three-hour lecture explaining why one plus one equals two. If they weren't in fact so basic that this example was complex in comparison.

I might have felt sorry for him for this very reason, if it hadn't been so obvious how teaching me things thrilled him, not to mention my progress during these years. And I knew that after I had introduced him to my brother, he had a worthy companion at least for more casual science. Thomas shared several of the traits which made Alex like me in the first place, and was skilful enough within his field that he could have an informed discussion with Alexis, something I knew the magician to appreciate more than anyone else would likely believe. But then they thought him to be a cruel lord of the abyss revelling in his superiority, and I knew better.

Alexis gently called me back into reality. "This is actually quite bad," he admitted, as he gave me a worried look. "Will you allow me to," I smiled as he had one of his small 'setbacks' and sounded like a satanic Jane Austen novel. And no, I do *not* mean *Pride and Prejudice AND ZOMBIES*. "Take you to my workshop?" I nodded. When he reached out a hand for me, I nodded again. I knew well what he meant; he wanted to carry me. And I let him.

He lifted me up, more carefully than anyone in the entire university would believe (possibly with the exception of my brother, who had connected some dots while they had been working together) and carried me quickly to his suite. If anyone saw us, they must have been looking *truly* closely.

I listened with great interest to a lecture far superior to those any other teacher of mine would make and allowed Alexis to care for my hand as he liked. Which probably was his intention in offering it. But I didn't mind being manipulated somewhat as long as he didn't try to *hide* the fact that he *was* manipulating me.

That was one of the things I liked best about Alex. He never hid things from me like that. Which was very nice after all intrigues that people (including Djinns, and vampires etc.) were constantly into. Even better had been if this no nonsense personality had been typical of angels in general, but I had never seen anything to make me believe that it was so. Hours had passed, most likely, and I had fallen asleep to the sound of Alexis singing. If I ever revealed to anybody that Alexis could sing, he would most likely kill somebody. Namely, the one I'd told.

An unassuming (and probably made by someone scared to death) knock on Alex's door awoke me. He opened it magically, and outside stood a young angel, Irria, wearing her usual downtrodden mien. I suspected that it came partly from how everyone always made her the messenger when it came to Alexis (unless I was available and took it on simply because I found them so silly) since she, being an angel, was much more difficult to cast spells over. It was just as *doable*, actually, but it took somewhat longer and thus she had more time to escape. But she was convinced that he hated her for having wings, and was just as terrified of him as the next person. This was mostly needless, of course, a great deal of the time, but they didn't know that. Nobody believed me when I assured them all sorts of things about my best friend, so I had stopped trying years ago.

"The headmaster wonders where the student – the pupil – you disappeared with earlier is," she advised him, visibly trying to find her courage.

"I had to repair the damage a healer who truly sucked (hearing him speak so strongly influenced by me made me giggle) caused, and now she is asleep, unless you've awoken her…" Alexis' tone was neutral, not at all aggressive, now when he wasn't provoked. Most everyone missed that detail about him.

The younger angel didn't miss it, though. She was still scared to death, but decided to say what she had to say anyway. "You shouldn't use your powers the way you do," she criticised him carefully, though firmly.

"Use them?" one side of Alexis' mouth quirked somewhat. "I have quite a temper," he surprisingly admitted, "I am easily annoyed when people around me act like idiots, which unfortunately isn't very uncommon, as it happens. But *use*? I could end lives daily and control everybody's business continuously, but I don't."

"Someone would put a stop to you then," she tried to make his argument invalid.

"Sure, naturally," Alexis agreed. "They would *try*. Are you really saying they *could*? I would have serious trouble for a full *hour*, I'm certain, but I could go for the cliché of ruling the world if I wanted to. It'd be easy. So *use*? Don't be silly," he said the last in a dismissing, finishing tone. But she was an angel, so she simply couldn't avoid snooping. Or if there was some other reason, beyond me. Although this question was fairly logical. And Alexis didn't look taken aback in the least.

"Then why aren't you?" she questioned.

Alexis shook his head and stretched. "Honestly speaking?" a smile surprised Irria, but not me. "That is for me to know, and for you to not. Now get lost," the door shut before her in a moment. I hoped that she didn't get hurt. Alexis, who knew me well enough to snap up these ponderings completely without the help of any mind reading, assured me, "She's fine." Since he more than knew that, and would never lie to me, I accepted this without question.

"How does it feel?" Alexis came over and sat down beside me on the day bed which I had never quite managed to figure out why he had. He rarely rested and slept only sporadically. Weird.

"May I move my fingers?" growing up at a university had awarded me with a healthy respect for disturbing anything magical, or scientific for that matter, mid through.

"Sure. Just be careful, this has been a quick one, but your hand is whole again," Alexis explained. The pain was entirely gone, of course, but suddenly my heart leapt into my throat. The once broken finger could move again, for the first time since I was four.

"What is it?" say what you will of Alex, he was never inattentive.

"My finger is moving!" I exclaimed. "My little finger is moving when I jiggle my fingers!" Alex laughed, but then looked lightly concerned. "Yes, you had some scar tissue that I removed for you. Was that all right?"

"Sure." I shook my head fondly and waved my little finger at him.

"You ought to go down for dinner, your brother must miss you," the magician decided with a laugh. "And I am off to the sick wing," he muttered.

"Absolutely not!" I objected and jumped down onto the floor. I was just about to elaborate on my protest when he shook his head.

"This is not about me being protective and hence pissed off," he explained. "The healer who healed you did a truly atrocious job of it. I have to do something about that before he hurts someone else."

I raised an eyebrow, "Grandmaster of magic, out to fix something? Man, you have spent far too much time with my brother."

A smile was hinted in one corner of the angel's mouth. "Not at all. It has always occurred now and again that I have helped correct things or other, and everybody is just as surprised every time. The truth is that either that idiot is so much a novice that I wonder at him being allowed to touch anyone at all, or he hurt you on purpose. In any case, I have to look this up." Alexis gave me a look and something glimmered in his eyes, "And that does not translate to tossing him off a balcony," he assured me.

"Why would anyone hurt me on purpose?" I questioned while we left Alex's workshop and headed for the stairs. "I am not a very good target."

"You have no enemies and nothing important rests on your shoulders, *yet*," Alexis gave me another look, one that completely gainsaid any statement about his cruelty, "nothing magical, anyway. But you are very close to two of the masters of this university. You are probably the simplest way of getting at your brother, and the *only* way to get at me. That makes you a target. Luckily, that also gives you yet more *awesome* forces on your side." I smiled in reply as he stressed my favourite word for describing magic.

Chapter 2

The dining hall was an enormous room, full of stone pillars and long wooden tables set with benches. Cross the dwarf halls in Moria with the great hall of Hogwarts and you'll be close enough. Thousands of people lived, studied and worked here, and the dining hall reflected those numbers. Slightly elevated in one end of the hall stood the head tables: one for the headmaster and teachers of the school, and one for the foremost magicians and scientists.

The headmaster sat at the seat of honour, at the very middle of one of them, and the other seat of honour was empty, as Alexis had decided to first visit the sick wing. My brother sat at the right side of the empty chair, partly because he was one of the foremost academics at the school, and partly because he simply dared to.

The chair at the left side of the place of honour, classically speaking the foremost place for a lady, had been mine since before my brother had gotten his fancy spot. Not because of my academic refinement, but because of the wishes of other academics. My brother had always insisted to keep me at his own table, a wish he already had been powerful enough to push through when I was a little girl, and since I had become friends with Alex it was only natural to put me next to him, as he rather scared most of the other candidates. My brother had sat at my other side for a long time.

"Where have you been, sister?" Thomas wondered as I had gotten a tray of food at the other end of the room and taken a seat at the head table. The rest of the academics within hearing looked up eagerly as they awaited the reply. They probably knew, all of them, that healing and Alexis would both be involved.

"I have been listening to an excellent lecture on the subject of substance-less magic," I replied to my brother and cut a crisply fried (it is good, but hell only knows how it's done) potato into pieces.

"Ah, and did you do your homework?" my brother visibly struggled with being a parent instead of leaping head first into the subject. He knew that the lecture probably contained things that he, too, wanted to know as he could guess the lecturer.

"Half, or thereabouts," I answered with a shrug, "I was interrupted. I will do the rest this evening." I thereafter devoted my attention to my food and let my brother continue a conversation about yellow magic with his present table neighbour where they had left it off.

Not twenty minutes later, just as I returned to the table with my second helping, the hall suddenly went about 80% less noisy; the typical reaction which heralded that Alexis had shown up for dinner. It wasn't only that he freaked people out, partly it was actually a respect deal. But mostly he just freaked them out.

Alexis waved one hand, and a plate filled itself with food and flew up into his hand. Most magicians rarely bothered with such things, since it was a waste of power, but for Alexis it was a matter of no effort, barely noticeable, in fact, so he didn't much care for that rule.

One of the silver goblets, set forward for the college and the masters of the various subjects, this one engraved with Alexis' personal coat of arms, filled itself with Fanta (he isn't half as old-fashioned as you'd think, even though he is so *old* he *has* a coat of arms in the first place) and flew elegantly up to the space beside me. Alex followed it. It was close to sixty metres walk through the hall to reach the head tables. They are the foremost places, but far from the most practical. Although, that connection is fairly common. Have you ever *seen* a ceremonial robe? Gorgeous, but completely impractical to even *walk* in, never mind function.

The academics at the head table moved their chairs to let him get through, despite the complete lack of need for that action, and he took the honorary seat of the table of masters with a simplicity which left no question about whether he belonged there or not. Some of the noise in the hall returned as he was seated, but most people within hearing range wanted to hear what we would say. Sometimes, people were all curious enough to be angels.

Alexis ruffled my hair and asked, "So, how is the hand now, little sparrow, hmm?" I smiled at him.

"I can move all my fingers!" Alexis actually laughed, to general surprise. It did not matter how often he actually laughed, everyone remained just as surprised anyway.

"It is well that I could be of some use, then," he replied, giving me a light nudge.

My brother took that opportunity to deflect the conversation towards knowledge. "My sister said that you gave her a lecture in the spirit of magic earlier today."

"Naaah," I teased, "I said *someone* did."

"And you called it interesting, so it was not very difficult to guess the lecturer," my brother teased right back.

"I did," Alexis replied courtly and winked at me before turning back to Thomas.

"Have you gotten any further in your studies of uses of unicorn hair within various fields and areas?"

My brother sighed, "No. I am stuck!" he struck his hands out in a despondent manner. "The only thing more impossible is the stages of regeneration of angels' wings!" my brother, and those who were still listening instead of having returned to their dinners, became little question marks when Alexis gave him a wide smile.

"That in particular, I have conducted extensive research on, as well as the possible roadblocks," he enlightened him. "I also have old research on unicorns which might help you out. Would you like a hand?"

My brother's smile almost split his face. "Certainly! What would you think about…"

"Not now!" Alexis stopped him lightly, a smile growing on his face. "We will bore your young sister to death. What say you of taking on the research after dinner?" My brother agreed. Not that it was actually a question, really.

Alexis turned back to me, "What did you think about the soul-snare I told you about before?" he wondered.

"Perilous and perilously boring," I shrugged, "which is an impressive combination." Alex gave a cold laughter.

"Not really. You actually have science, and magic, for that matter, in a nutshell there. When it comes to theory, anyways."

Like any scientists, despite Alexis' continuous protests that he wasn't one, they went to work with their knowledge at the very first opportunity. I looked on without interest from my place at the small inside balcony opposite the one outside my brother's bedroom, and wasn't even listening with one ear. I moved my right hand's fingers with fascination. I could suddenly move them all again, and I couldn't even remember what that feeling felt like. I remembered very little from back when I was that young.

Instead, possibly conjured by the image of my 'family' below, or perhaps the presence of Alexis, I pondered a few slightly later childhood memories instead. Alexis was part of surprisingly many of those.

At Another Time

It was the 17th. Kiera sobbed slightly. She remembered the last time it was the 17th only too well. It had been her eleventh birthday. Her father had been baking a cake sprinkled with chocolates and, despite him and her mother naturally being at each other's throats as always, they made more of an effort than normal to keep their voices down for her. It didn't matter too much. Her brother had come home from his school, the 'university' and brought her presents. It had been unusually cosy in the little purple kitchen. Kiera gave another sob. This time, they were both gone. Mum and Dad, even the house itself.

She was disrupted from her thoughts by someone. He said nothing, but she could feel him there. Her brother had explained it to her a week earlier, as she had first got there, to the university, that certain people, the ones with a lot of magic, could be *felt* like that.

While she looked up, slowly, the man, who was wearing jeans and a black shirt, had crouched down before her, and their eyes suddenly met. His eyes had the same mystical colour as the flames of a really hot fire. "Who are you?" she asked.

He beat her question to it with one tenth of a second. "What is the matter?" their words collided, but neither of them smiled. He waited for her to go first. When she didn't, he gave a troubled smile, encouraging, "ladies first!"

"*Everything* is the matter!" Kiera answered with yet another sob, instinctively throwing herself around the neck of the man. This didn't seem to worry him, though if she could have seen his face, she would have been able to read surprise on it. But nobody could. They were in a rather forgotten hallway and entirely alone.

The man sat down where Kiera had been sitting, still holding the sobbing child, before answering her question. "My name is Alexis," he explained kindly, apparently to take her mind off her tears. "Alexis Darn. Like the cuss word!" Kiera looked at him with her thoroughly wet eyes. Her brother had warned her about the magician Alexis Darn, but he seemed very nice to her. Neither did he look like she expected. Weren't magicians supposed to have capes (although she didn't actually know what those looked like) and look very serious?

Alexis Darn was tall, especially from Kiera's point of view, but not at all as tall as some others at the university, and the general impression was that he looked very dark, though with a closer inspection there was nothing to warrant the impression.

His hair was pitch black, and he looked tanned, especially for spring, but not exceptionally so. Maybe that ungraspable first impression of darkness was simply the shadow of an angel without wings. The hair, which curled around his shoulders but otherwise was straight, looked like it had never ever seen a comb, ever, but instead had been utterly forgotten.

"And who are you?" he asked the question very carefully.

"My name is Kiera. It is from a book," she added, like her mum always did before. Then, since her brother had told her she was always supposed to if any of the academics asked who she was, she noted, "I am the little sister of Thomas Sparrow, who studies the 'transformation of species'." Since she did not really know how that was supposed to help anyone understand anything, she added just one more thing, "I live with him now. Our parents are gone."

"Oh dear," was the opinion of Alexis. "First, you lose your parents, then you have to come live with a bunch of boring professors. You poor little one!" the last part seemed mostly meant for himself, and it seemed to Kiera that it was more thoughtful than meant as pity. Kiera liked that.

The angel looked at her for a moment and then wondered out loud, "Would you like to join me in my workshop? I could show you some magic that isn't so boring!" He had lifted her out of his lap now, and rose. After hesitating for half a second, he reached out a hand to her.

Kiera hesitated too. Her whole life, she had been told—especially by her father—how she was not supposed to talk to strangers, and certainly not follow them anywhere. *Especially,* not men. Although when she came here, her brother had loosened that rule, explaining that he knew most people here, and said that at university, she was allowed to talk to anyone she wanted, and as long as someone else knew where she was, she could walk to places with them, too. On the other hand, he had warned her of the magician Darn.

Alexis, who didn't even know himself why he smiled in a friendly fashion, or even less what made him feel he ought to care for this sad little girl, patiently awaited her decision. He was a very insightful and observant man, and either way truly didn't believe in rushing things. Out of his three favourite characters, in any category in books, one of them was actually *Skalman*. "Hurry up" was certainly not an expression he took to using lightly.

Regardless, if it was the fact that no one stressed her about it, or if she just found him to be kind-looking, she decided her super-old big brother could not always be right. She skipped up off the stone bench she had been sitting on and took Alexis's hand, while she asked, "Why are there stone benches inside?"

"That's an old university thing," Alexis confided in her and then looked down on the child with a smile of mutual understanding. "It is weird and wonky, isn't it?"

Alexis made some of his enchanted cocoa for the first time in years, and watched the girl from a distance as she peeked around his workshop. Just like lots of the academics of the university, he lived on top of his workshop, but otherwise things were slightly different.

Firstly, his jointly magic and scientific place was positively huge, he actually had an entire annex at his service; secondly, he was not very liberal with whom he invited, or even admitted here. Especially not beyond the spacious atria, where he sometimes worked and preferred to meet with academics and other magicians if he at any time found it worthwhile to cooperate with them. Which was not all that often.

Kiera was strolling around looking at everything. She had believed that all 'scientists' at this place lived like her brother, but apparently that wasn't true. Thomas had a large, light bedroom opening up onto an inside balcony overlooking his workshop, to which you got by way of a ladder.

The workshop itself consisted of a room with bookshelves covering every inch of the high walls, barely leaving enough space for the door. Besides their numbers, they were all almost full, which she thought was a peculiarity as all the books seemed to be spread across the carpet and her brother's desk instead.

This workshop was different. The ceiling was almost as high, but the bookshelves were spread out, and only reached the high ceiling on one wall. It was much larger than her brother's, and contained a lot of things which she didn't even need to be told not to touch.

"Those are angel feathers," Alexis enlightened her, as he came up to her with two large cups of hot cocoa. He gave her the black one and kept the blue for himself. Kiera turned around eagerly enough that she almost spilled her hot chocolate. "What are those for?" she asked pointing to several pliers lying spread across the tabletop.

"I make dream catchers out of them, the feathers, then they really will protect you from bad dreams," he explained kindly.

After a moment of hesitation, Alexis put his cup down on the bench and pulled out a high, but comfortable and steady, desk chair from somewhere. He placed the girl, who was standing on her tiptoes to be able to look up at the bench, which was the right high for him to stand and work by, onto the chair and in the same movement slid it in. Then he stood next to her to show her how it was done.

Kiera glared at the man. "You cannot lift me up without asking first!" she objected. Alexis looked at her, without showing any surprise.

"I'm sorry," he said sincerely instead. "I am not used to asking. But I will remember, I promise."

"Uhrm," Kiera's reply was barely approving.

Half an hour later, they were in the middle of making a dream catcher, and Alexis was just showing her how to attach the feathers. "First, pierce them with the silver thread, that way it will stick better," the magician instructed. When he saw the accident about to happen, as the girl would inevitably prick her fingers, he instantaneously pierced the base of all the feathers himself with the help of magic.

The girl looked at the feather she was holding with fascination. "How did you do that?"

Alexis smiled at her, "I did promise you that not all magic was boring, didn't I!"

Chapter 3

"Kiera!" my brother stood outside in the workshop, calling. I could bet that he, just at the last minute, adjusted something he had forgotten. My bedroom was one of the rooms placed beneath Thomas's inside balcony and bedroom. It was painted the blue-green colour of tropical water, and it was a book-free zone.

"I am awake—I will head to my lessons when they *begin*!" I assured him tiredly. Sometimes, I was sick and tired of my absent-minded big brother's attempts at being a good parent. When lots of rattle and finally a door had assured me that my brother had skedaddled to start the day with a scientific discussion, I looked around my bedroom.

It wasn't very big, but not small either. My bed, which was large and round, dominated the space with its crimson sheets and the frankly enormous quilt I used for a bedspread.

One wall was half hidden behind a huge wardrobe, and two smaller chests stood up against the other side. Only one of them actually contained clothes and fabrics and stuff. In the middle of the ceiling, above the bed, a large dream catcher, made by silver, suede and angel feathers was hung. One feather, very large and white, hung furthest down. It came from Alexis himself. If he had still had his wings, they would clearly have been of the impressive, beautiful kind. Even compared to any angel's wings.

I walked between my bedroom and my en suite to get ready for the morning. Then I pulled on my favourite jeans and gave my schedule a quick look as I buttoned my bra.

10:15 Advanced magical theory
11:45 Complicated magic usage
14:15 Magical craft, exam preparation course

Both of my pre-noon lessons were of the advanced kind, actually they were the finishing lessons of their set, despite the fact that I was only seventeen, since I had started to study at the university just before I turned twelve. My brother had given me some of the help I had needed to reach such a level, but mostly it was Alexis who had prepared me, and he still gave me a fair amount of lessons and support. I was always in the top of the class when it came to results, even though I was about a decade younger compared to most of my classmates.

Since my brother did not have a normal concept of mornings, he had awakened me at a quarter to six, which when combined with my very unfeminine (to classicists and sexists, anyway) ability to always get ready within twenty minutes, had given that I was not exactly in a hurry.

I settled down on the carpet and opened up my course book in theory. Alexis and I had spent an entire week going through it, and I had read it myself as well. This meant that I now had only a dozen pages or so left and knew all of it almost by heart.

I laid down, getting comfortable while I looked for the right page. I did not look up before I had read through the entire rest of the book, but when I had, I gave the clock a slightly nervous look. I might be seriously suspicious against books in general, but they still had a tendency to grasp me. It was a quarter past seven o'clock.

I placed the book tidily into the pile of things I needed for my pre-noon lectures, and picked up my practically oriented course literature instead. This book I did not need Alexis to help me with, but since I had focused on the other one, I had only gotten halfway through it as of yet. I allowed myself to tilt over and fall onto the carpet with the intention to do something about it.

A knock on the door interrupted me, and it was almost with a degree of shock I realised that I had read well past a hundred pages. The practical book was for obvious reasons not such a brick as the theoretical one, so I only had about forty pages left of the entire thing. "Come in," in my worry about maybe being late I couldn't find my watch, so when

Alexis stepped into the room I looked at him worriedly. "What time is it?"

"Half past nine." He gave me an amused look, "Got stuck in the world of books?" he shook his head in criticism, but the glitter in his eyes was merely teasing.

"I am finishing off course literature," I informed him and got up with a yawn.

Alexis smirked, "Well, you have to do that sometime," he supposed. He handed me a folder I recognised well. It was my red theory one. "I looked at the theoretical quotes you'd made and corrected a few spelling errors," he smiled. "This is all right now. Tease your teacher and hand it in already."

I accepted it with a smile. "Don't get yourself late reading," the angel admonished me before he let himself out. I opened the folder and rested it against my knee. The essay looked exactly like it did when I had handed it away—the only thing Alexis had done was, as usual, exactly what I had asked him to.

The subject was classical reasons of overusing magic, yet another of the magic sectors where Alexis was one of the most recognised experts. I had included conclusions and quotes from four other academics, including my brother, but mostly relied on Alex as a source.

I had quoted him carelessly, and sometimes deliberately left gaps, only to then ask him to fill in the blanks. I knew that all of them would be found in one of the books he published every year, probably the books of magical advice. If nothing else, in this year's edition of the latter. Nobody had missed that I had inside information, so me having access to his new, unpublished writings would raise no eyebrows.

I put the folder into the pile of things which was going into the school bag, and upon closer thought, I packed everything except the book on practical magic, which I was absorbed in as I went down to eat breakfast in the dining hall.

Four hours later, I closed the book with a bang and tucked it down into my bag. I had read during the entirety of my lunch break and now had only half an hour left until my afternoon lesson. And I had not eaten lunch yet. I would probably do best to hurry up.

Stood in the dining hall were several groups of anxious new students, all of them a few years older than I was myself, looking on with fascination as a thoughtful Alexis got the chairs at the head table, where he currently sat alone, to fly around. It could have been called a nervous habit—providing, of course, that it had anything even remotely to do with nerves. It didn't.

Since I was in no way as impressed as the older beginners, I went and looked at what food was served. The food at the University was usually pretty inspiring, but evidently today they had run out of ideas. Or they didn't want to spoil the newly arrived pupils already on the second day, perhaps.

I abandoned the solid foods and peeked into the always-present soup which always looked like someone's vomited lunch from yesterday. This was just as true today as it was any other day. But I, who had lived here long enough to have made a few discoveries, knew it to be very good if you only dared to try it out. And I wasn't exactly known to be a chicken—if nothing else I *was* Alexis Darn's best friend. I had some soup.

The beginners stared at me as I squeezed ahead of them, and I heard whispers, all about my age, except one or two criticising that I would leave the group on the first day. I went straight on ahead to the head table, leaving them dead silent. First out of horror, then admiration when they realised that I was actually meant to sit there. When Alexis dropped all the chairs to enthusiastically greet me, their jaws almost literally hit the floors.

"Well, hello there, lilla sparv,"[1] Alexis noted and gave me a warm embrace as soon as I had put my plate down. "It was terribly dreary here when you were gone!"

"Now I have finished my course literature, anyway, so I suppose I will be slightly more present," I joked.

---

[1] A small note on translations: 'lilla sparv' is a phrase in a language Alexis met during the years of his long lifetime that are unknown to us; the words translate to 'little sparrow'.

Alexis raised one eyebrow, "You have a full semester left on your course, lilla sparv." It was Monday, eleventh of January, the first day of the semester, and Alexis was just being foolish. I was to take my magical exams in two days' time.

"I have decided to start another subject, after my exam on craft on Friday," I told him with enthusiasm. I had found out for sure during the day, in between lessons. "Advanced magical creatures."

"Yes," Alexis answered randomly and I turned towards him with some surprise, looking up from my soup. I knew him well enough for it to be obvious that he had just replied to a question, but it was not one I had asked.

Luckily, Alex was kind enough to explain himself, at least a little. "Yes," he elaborated, "you may interview me when you get to searching out magical creatures and reach angels," he grinned to me, "that is the hardest part of the entire course." I laughed so that I almost got the soup back up, not that anyone would have noticed. There was something somewhat ironic about how the soup generally known as 'vomit soup' tasted so good.

"How do you think your exam will turn out?" the magician changed the subject. I shrugged and thought about all the energy we had jointly put into my last courses during the Yule break.

"I know I will pass."

Alexis gave me a small smile, "Probably you will get excellent grades and finish at the top of your class."

"I am good," I admitted, "but I am no star pupil."

Alexis shrugged, "No, you are not your brother, but when it comes to magic craftsmanship, you are one of the best that I know of. Looking at the whole of the subject, you have your teachers beat. And then some," he lifted a chair by way of a barely distinguishable movement of one finger alone. "And that is not so strange considering how you have been active at the level you have since you were eleven."

I didn't bother asking what he meant. With time, I had realised that the angel-feather dream catchers I had helped

Alex to make as a child was an exceedingly advanced form of magic, which only masters dabbled in. And Alexis had taught me before I even started my studies at the university. Hell, I still had the occasional trouble with my shoelaces at the time!

I had jumped headfirst into what I wanted to know, already then, guided by my curiosity. I started in January with the new semester exactly six years ago, and read the same three subjects as I progressed from beginner's level to very advanced. The magical ground which I had chosen was for six years, the first half of a dozen as so much was within the studies of magic, but craft magic was seven. I had taken in a full year. Really more considering that most did not get through the background of that profession in less than seven and a half years. Even eight was fairly frequent. Ah, well. We are all good at something.

I got up from the table, leaving the soup plate where it was, since I was starting to be in a hurry for my second to last lecture ever in my favourite subject. Besides, I knew Alexis would send it off to the right place as he disposed of his own.

I spent the evening and the next day studying in a way I could not recall ever having done before. I was used to studying in a pretty laidback fashion, but now I had started to grow nervous. I assumed it was the natural reaction to one of the most important exams of my life, no matter how many degrees I would afterwards decide to take.

If I made this, I would be a basic mage, then a crafting one. And, as they were thirteen years together, a magician. It was an impressive education for anyone, even excluding the fact that I shouldn't even have started at the university yet. Most didn't study two such subjects in parallel, either, but had basic magical or academic degrees for many years during their education, but they had neither my backup, nor my very weird childhood.

My head was entirely empty, in a foggy, tired fashion. I left my first exam after a full day in the exam hall, and almost walked into my brother and Alexis, both of whom met me outside. "So, how does it feel!" my brother was all enthusiasm, and his face clearly told me he knew exactly what it felt like.

Alexis, who had gotten all his degrees (he had run out of subjects) a considerably longer time ago, contented himself with patting one of my shoulders.

The Thursday started with Alexis waking me at 10:30 by knocking at my door. It was apparently an exam that was needed for my brother to not wake me at dawn. "No lessons today, just preparations," Alexis reminded me as I had dressed and accompanied him through the university towards the dining hall. "I suggest that you bring whatever you need to my workshop, and I will help you as best as I can whenever you need it," he looked positively nervous himself. "If there still is something you ponder over or do not know, this is the time to ask," he reminded me.

The Friday exam felt exactly like my first one, afterwards, even if the process itself was different. Alexis met me this time as well, but my brother did not. This exam itself wasn't as important, only the degree was. Now, it was all about waiting.

I had walked through mist the entire first week of the semester, figuratively speaking, and the weekend I had spent with Alexis in his workshop. They were always quick to correct this type of exams, and a mix of magic and the rather manageable number of students at this level allowed them to be. There was no doubt that I would know my results as early as Monday. I preferred to bide my time until then.

On Monday morning, I didn't just rise, but unusually left my brother's apartment already at half past six. I went straight to the academic's presidium, where we got to pick up our exam results and degrees. Their chief of something I could never remember, who was of the very early rising sort, greeted me kindly. "You are up early," she smiled.

I smiled back, "Not much earlier compared to usual, but I normally stay in and read in the mornings," I admitted.

"No wonder that was impossible today," she agreed with understanding and got my new results out for me.

I opened them up right away, my hands trembling.

Basic degree in magic, direction set magical theory and magic usage.

Kiera Tallion Sparrow
New basic mage
Exemplary

I stared at the paper, at the signatures under the text and the seals. Not only was it real, it was good, as well. A small list on an attached paper enlightened me of the general grades which I already knew by heart after many years of hearing them listed and talked about in the halls. As always, they were listed vertically with the best grades on top and the worst down below. There were half a dozen of approved grades. What else.

Masterful
Exemplary
Inspirating
Skilful
Very satisfactory
Reliable
Worthy of a second chance
Unworthy, but justified of, a second chance
Guilty of nerves
Incompetent
Sad
Entertaining
Quite silly

My grade, which as of my other studies would be a master of magic degree, was like a silver then, essentially. The woman watched me with a small smile and reminded me about the other envelope. I ripped it open.

Specialised degree in magic – creative magic

Kiera Tallion Sparrow
Master of magic
Masterful

I stared equally as hard at this paper. Just as Alexis had thought, I had reached a perfect result. What I had left now, on a higher level, were advanced degrees of magic, things like the title of 'higher master' which demanded half a dozen titles or possibly grandmaster of magic which meant a full dozen of titles and which needed, respectively, half a century of studies and several centuries of studies. I didn't quite aim there.

I interrupted Alexis in the middle of an experiment which probably didn't have all that much of a purpose anyway, as it was based upon flying fruits, and almost tossed my results onto him. He gave me a warm hug.

Since I was hesitant about disturbing my very serious brother in the middle of his science, I waited until dinner to tell him. And after dinner came the ceremony to name new basic mages and new masters. Or in my case (I was the only one) both.

By Tuesday, the everyday finally started again. Thomas woke me up at half past five for no real reason and I spent the morning reading through about half of my new course literature, before I, at ten o'clock, went to my first lesson in the new subject I had chosen. It had basic mage as requirement, which in practice meant that I was amongst those eight to ten years my seniors, with lower degrees by far. Fun. And somewhat *fun* with the weight on sarcasm.

Chapter 4

"You have three lessons per week," Alexis noted, suddenly. It was the Friday of the week in which I had received my degree, and we were sitting in his workshop. I looked up from the toy train I had enchanted into driving round a small wooden set of rails all on its own. I silently waited for him to elaborate and become slightly more specific.

"You study far less compared to before, what with your basic degree dealt with and a considerably less complex subject, even though in no way an easy one," Alexis continued by way of explanation, "and you have nothing else you'd like to study on the side, you did that already!" He grinned. "You are even through your entire list of readable classic literature. What are you going to do with your time?"

I smiled in reply and admitted sheepishly, "I kinda had in my head that now when I had taken my degrees, everything would become more difficult, but that isn't really right, is it? There's nothing I want to study on the levels above mine, I already settled my own field, and... well, I don't know," I answered truthfully.

"What about instead reading something on the levels *below*?" Alexis asked unexpectedly. "Read a basis in something else." I looked at him in surprise. I guessed that he had a reason, and I was curious of what that was. Besides that, it was a little unexpected, even random.

"If you started to read something independent, less advanced, you would end up with the new students," Alexis explained. "Kiera, you will soon turn eighteen, but at the moment you are actually only seventeen, and starting to study here at nineteen is very special." He looked at me with warmth in his fire-blue eyes. "You are very, very good, but you never once had your own age around you. If you ever did, it was a very long time ago. Before I even met you. Do you not think that now would be the time to try it out? And something at a more basic level, just for inspiration, would be good for you."

"Are you trying to get rid of me?" I was merely teasing, and he shook his head, smiling. "What are you suggesting?" I wondered, curious.

"What about any of the basic 'studies'?" Alexis suggested willingly. "You could start there with magic beings, although I suspect that'd be boring, it is better if you get some change. What about the study of feathers or feather magic, or the study of appearances of magical creatures? The latter is too close too, I would guess…"

"The 'study' on angels, perhaps?" I suggested. I was teasing, but his answer was casual, not moved by it.

"Yes, why not," said Alex.

I restarted the conversation after a few minutes of silence, in which we both dealt with ours, which in his case meant sowing tomato plants. He turned his eyes to me again. "Why do you frighten so many people, but are so kind to me?" I knew I had asked him something similar as a child, and on all accounts, got an excellent reply. But I didn't remember it.

"I am nice to you because I like you," was the honest, and earnest, response. "I am a man with far too much temper and far too few consequences if I do not rein it in. But I am not evil, or even mean, in the end. Some dark humour, a few idiots too many around me and too little actual company." He shrugged a little at this point, "There you have it."

"A little too much experience, too, maybe," I suggested. "Yes, you might be right there," he concurred. Then he went to wipe off his earthy hands and make some chocolate. Sometimes the simplest logic is the wisest. Actually, surprisingly often.

It had been twelve days since Alexis had healed my hand. Since the whole and half dozen, as well as thirteen, had such importance within magic, or rather within magic society, (if there actually was some real magical importance then I had never noticed) I should have known all hell would break lose.

The day had been normal enough. I had already gotten straight through my new course literature, currently in study overdrive, and I had spent the rest of the morning experimenting alongside Alexis. It was during the afternoon, when I, yet unaware of the approaching emergency, cleaned up amongst my notes and sorted the past ones into their new places in the big chest, as things started to happen.

While I was placing my red and blue folders away safely with my old school books, to instead place a new green folder and my three new (though read) books about magical beings into my bag, Alexis was up to no good. Well, *kinda*.

I went down to have dinner, but it seemed to have been rather abruptly cancelled. Quite a few magicians and members of the teachers' staff had gathered in the middle of the great dining hall, having an organised argument (which was by far the best, not to say only, description of that meeting I can give).

On one side stood members from the medical staff, three of whom were hanging upside down, on another side stood several professors, in the middle were a couple more teachers, and the headmaster. Somewhat for himself, but still in the middle of the hall, stood Alexis and watched them argue. I tiptoed up to my brother, standing with several other academics somewhat to one side. I did not even need to ask.

"It seems as if some of the healer apprentices have been planning some illegal activities. And we're speaking rebel stuff for direction," my brother whispered by way of explanation. I raised my eyebrows in surprise.

"So you're saying that my students were planning to *attack* the university?" the chief of the healers exploded.

"*Yes!*" someone else supplied quickly.

"And how would they ever think they could pull that off?" the Headmaster criticised, obviously trying to calm things down.

General silence ensued as Alexis replied, "They didn't. They would never manage, which they knew." He turned quietly to the headmaster. That Alexis could go into a rage when the right buttons were pushed was hardly a secret, but an argument wasn't gonna shake him.

"As I told you earlier in the week, one of the healers hurt young master Kiera Sparrow about two weeks ago. I am sure you remember that she hurt herself quite badly at a fall and needed medical attention." Some of the academics looked ready to stop Alexis's monologue, perhaps to question the relevance of these seemingly rather random statements, but no one dared to.

"This was a conscious fault, however, it was an isolated event," Alexis continued methodically. "I checked; there was no one else hurt by the healers in this way. Why her in particular? Well, they knew they could not take on all the many competent magicians living here at once so they came up with a plan. They decided to use the corrupt spell to kill young Sparrow, and hoped that I would do so for them. It was really a *terribly* bad plan."

The silence was still compact, in the middle of the raging argument. No one seemed up to discuss it with Alexis, certainly no one was volunteering, so I decided to take him on myself. Again.

"Why?" I stepped up and asked. All eyes turned on me, then back once again to Alex.

He looked at me kindly. "It is quite right that I could do something properly nasty, for revenge, or whatever, should anyone hurt you. I take friendship very seriously, *you* know that," he started. "But that is just half of a relationship. They missed the other side."

I waited silently for the continuation. I wasn't alone. Alex suddenly granted me a wide smile. "I am sure you can enlighten us on how it would be to die from a distorted healing-charm, master Sparrow," he continued.

"What?" was the immediate response from my brother, followed promptly by, "oh, this will take some time getting used to." Alexis was the only one to give a chuckle at that. I thought personally it was a blessing that *someone* could show a suitable sense of humour.

"It would hurt," I answered instead.

"Naturally, but above all it would take a lot of *time*," Alexis pointed out. I gave a nod in agreement. I wasn't alone now either. "What would you do if something strange and painful, obviously magical, suddenly happened to your injured hand?" he questioned further.

I smiled, "I would come to you for help."

He smiled back, "Exactly. And I would help you. And *then*, I would get absolutely pissed off and probably do something fairly violent to whoever was responsible."

"That's a bad plan, then," was my brother's rather unexpected input, "if it wasn't constructed by someone secretly seeking to get rid of the rebels."

"It would still be far from brilliant, because Kiera would never let me get rid of them properly," Alexis finished insightfully. The silence in the hall lasted even though the magician had stopped speaking and grown silent. The headmaster looked to be pondering what he was expected to say.

The woman who had given me my exam results earlier in the week suddenly spoke up. "Well, if we are certain they are guilty, they're going down for it. Do we know for sure that young Sparrow is their only victim? How is she doing now?" Alex nodded for reply as far as the first two questions were concerned, (even the one which was technically really more of a statement anyway) he was sure to know he spoke truly after his highly qualified (since it was *his*) research into the case and I answered the last one myself.

"Alexis healed me," I said for a reminder. "There's certainly nothing wrong with me now."

When it came down to it, everybody listened to Alexis when he unusually enough did get involved in things at the university, and for once was actually willing to contribute with his considerable expertise. The guilty parties, who Alexis kindly had already turned upside down, which helped, were locked up, their teacher was distraught, and we could finally have dinner.

Had this been performed by anyone else than Alexis, this would not have been the end of the story. But now, it was

Alexis who had taken on things, which meant it was done with when he said it was. Which was a very good quality of his. It is sometimes seriously awesome to have magicians for friends. And brothers... and staring at you from your mirror. Okay, that one's weird. Seriously funky, actually.

I spent a particularly exciting (not) Friday night listening to my brother turn the pages of his heavy books and researching which basic level class I ought to sign up for. I went to bed only at four am and hoped that my brother would remember that it was the weekend and not awaken me at five o'clock for once.

This was fairly rare, but when I woke by myself past ten, I realised it had still happened. Until I heard voices outside and realised my brother was simply busy with something academic which had made him forget the rest of the world quite effortlessly.

When I, at half past ten, came out into the workshop/library/living room, dressed in jeans and a tank-top with a cosy hoodie over it, I found my deeply fascinated brother, and Alexis, the latter lecturing about the regenerative ability of angel's wings, and simultaneously explained how the feathers were constructed. He sat with an enormous, white feather in one hand.

Only one of them turned around when I entered, or exited, the room and came towards them. "Good morning," my friend the storm-magician greeted me. "How is your first weekend as a magician?" My brother flinched at the change of subject, and it was obvious that he had just drastically returned to reality.

"Oh, good morning, little sister," he greeted me absentmindedly.

Alexis glanced at the beautiful silver clock he carried in a charm bracelet across one wrist. "It is past time for some breakfast, I think," he noted. My brother sighed. 'Master Sparrow' hated when ordinary human things took precedence over his studies. But it was probably good for him to be forced out into the world once in a while. Otherwise, he would sit with his books driving himself insane.

Thomas spent the entirety of the magnificent Saturday breakfast staring down into his plate and thinking. I assumed that he was processing what Alexis had told him and was waiting for the continuation. Alexis and I discussed putting spells on models, as in sculptures or toys, in the shape of for example animals so that they would get the abilities of what they portrayed. Put a spell on a crib mobile with seagulls so that they truly flew, for example.

It was one of the disciplines within crafting magic which created the most chaos were it misused, and Alexis took every chance he got to explain both basics within the subject as well as details to me. Although, today we mostly got into how much fun you could have with that type of magic if you didn't get yourself into trouble. "And what do you do if a problem *does* arise?" Alexis questioned me. I smiled in reply and speared some bacon, half a mushroom and a little bit of tomato onto my fork.

"I'll *scream* for you and my brother." With this he was satisfied. Me too; having Alex nearby was a supremely powerful lifeline.

I stayed at the table as Alexis allowed himself to be drawn back into my brother's workshop. Thomas might seem very absent-minded and mild when he was doing his thinking thing, but he too, was a force of nature. A gust of wind to Alexis's hurricane, granted, but considering Alex that was still fairly good work.

I was preoccupied with figuring out six separate ways of enchanting my fork, when I noticed that Dhrar had appeared on the other side of the table. Had it been a certain angel grand magician it might have actually been a genuine *appearance*, but in this case it was rather me being very inattentive.

"Hi!" I greeted Dhrar enthusiastically. Because of the chaos of the last two weeks, I had close to misplaced the majority of my friends. And if you wanted help with exam studies, Alexis kind of stood out as a rather obvious first choice.

"Congratulations, little master!" Dhrar said with a wide smile. "But where have you been the *last* week?"

"Getting used to a completely new schedule," I replied and went around the table with my empty plate. "It will take time to get used to it; that I am done now. There is no more complicated continuation to craft magic, not besides the education I am already receiving from Alex, anyway, and I am not interested in any higher, purely theoretical, magical education. At least, not now."

Dhrar looked at me in shock. "Then what will you *do*?" Hir, annoyingly, obviously thought of me as an academic who had ceased to study, and those stories *always* ended as tragedies of the first degree.

"I am taking on a new subject. Magical creatures, this time," I answered as I put my empty dishes away.

"Ah," the Djinn first looked relieved, then enthusiastic. "Well, that ought to suit you," hir noted. "Aside from craft magic I'd say it is the very best fit for you, out of anything." Hir's smile widened, "You do truly have a talent for choosing your subjects!"

I laughed while we walked through the main hallway, out of the dining hall, "Thanks!"

I hastily placed a hand on Dhrar's shoulder and asked, "Wait for me, I will be right back," when I saw the person I knew I needed to talk to. The djinn asked no questions (big advantage with them compared to angels) as I joined hir again, and we continued up to the open library.

There were two large, non-private libraries, in two entirely separate places inside the university walls. One of them, where I had only rarely been as I had other places to study and other sources to learn from compared to most others, was almost as large as the dining hall and was permanently to be in a state of utter silence.

The library we were heading for was of another type entirely. The younger inhabitants of the university, mostly new human students but also an entirely different type of residents of this place, like most of the less ancient djinns, preferred to hang out there.

Activities ranging all the way between readings to pool were common, and the silence rule was not all that strict either.

"Don't shout, someone might actually be reading a book worth its paper, but that's hardly likely, so laugh all you'd like." Or thereabouts.

"Wow, hello there magician!" yawped one of the younger djinns as we entered. Hir name was Charl and hir seemed to live in a permanent state of some sort of high (without any source we had found, anyway) which reminded some of us of the pirate films' Jack Sparrow. The djinn, who like any djinn could not easily be sorted into the boxes of male or female, went under several names amongst those much too human to be able to handle a typical djinn name like Charl. Charles and Charlotte were the most common, but I had also heard Charlotta, Chili and Charley regularly. I liked Chili myself. Somehow, that seemed the least misinformed.

I laughed at Charl's antics, and got a proper bear hug from Robin's sibling, Alex. I always mixed that Alex up with Alexis when I talked, but that was properly a personal problem of mine, as the name Alexis was barely used, never mind a well-known, but entirely private nickname between me and the magician. But *I* had issues with it!

I gave djinn-Alex an extra look as hir let go of me. Djinns, angels and humans all had different manners of dress, but Alex and Robin both were generally very un-djinnish djinns, not following the djinn fashion (if you could really call ancient traditions by that name) one bit. Now, on the other hand, Alex was dressed just like Dhrar, in clothes that aside from the trousers were draped around the body. That hir carried an amulet around the neck was normal, all djinns always did that to help channel their power properly, but no djinns who were even a least bit modern ever wore magical stones the way hir now did. Not even traditionalist Dhrar. What was the matter with Alex today? And Robin, with the traditional skin-tight braids in hir newly cut hair wasn't much better. Were those two even born when those traditions were generally followed?

The djinns, as usual, lounged in one of the couches which wasn't actually there, but I shook my confusing thoughts out of my head and smiled wickedly. Then I nonchalantly sat down in a chair that didn't exist either, and cockily crossed my legs. Alexis had taught me the spell the weekend before, while I had been trying not to think of how I had done in my exams.

"Impressive," Robin's sister (that was what Robin always said, anyway. I would wait until I am a master of djinn lore before analysing that particular point) commented teasingly, "but how long can you keep it up?"

Dhrar snorted, "Don't try to show off, Alex. That is one of grandmaster Darn's spells. Bet you, it is static now and will not need any more power from her." Quite right. In your face!

Chapter 5

"Did you hear?" and then a stressed, "Bye then, Kiera!" I glanced at the clock standing on the clothes chest standing nearest to the bed. Ten past *five*. Thomas had seriously outdone himself today. I turned onto my side, but as usual going back to sleep was completely impossible.

It was about five minutes past half past five as I stepped out into my brother's library. Already as a child, I had spent very little time sleeping, and it had not, despite everybody's predictions, straightened itself out in my early teenage years. My own theory was that it *would* have, if my brother's silly habit of always waking me so early hadn't entirely infiltrated my very bone marrow by then.

Five minutes later, I had to admit that Alexis was right. I had too little to study these days. What was I supposed to do with my time when I had neither the infamously difficult craft's magic nor my basic degree to busy myself with? My short-term solution was to go and eat breakfast.

After an out of pure habit involuntarily quick breakfast, I went for the more study oriented library and read a full book before I realised that it was about time to head for the first lesson in the subject I had hastily signed up for the day before. The study of angels. Basic level.

I started to feel hesitant before I even entered the classroom. Alexis was right, it had been ages since I had spent any amount of time with anyone my own age. Had I even spoken to a teenager in my entire life? Of course, my brain helpfully supplied the answer. *Thomas, when you were little.* Perfect.

Since this course was aimed more towards those without any degree than to those who had them, it had already been running for two weeks, instead of one. But the early times always came with some hassle, and I was not the only new face. Though almost.

Several conversations were up and going, awaiting the arrival of our teacher, but they were not in the least bit alike the focused exchanges of tasks and sound advice to which I was accustomed, or the professors' conversations about the weather which I had never been able to pinpoint *why* they were humorous (but they *were*).

"Hi!" a girl with red hair burst out as I sat next to her. I nodded in reply. "Are you new? Have you taken any courses here before? If not, let me warn you—we get terribly much homework!" the words flooded from her.

I silently stared at her for several seconds without replying. So long that several others noticed me. I remembered, I did, complaints about homework and tasks from little school, but it felt so *distant*. These weren't little children, they were all in their twenties. Why did they study if they didn't like it? I realised with an internal sigh that I suddenly had ended up far beyond the absurd academics' thoroughly curious world.

"But, aren't you a bit young to study here?" a tall guy with blond hair questioned. Before I could explain or even answer (or run the hell away), our teacher appeared. I had studied alongside her a long time ago, some part of magic theory, when she was getting ready for her basic magical degree. Her education was ten or eleven years, was my guess. Mine was worth thirteen. That just couldn't be good.

She broke our conversation short with a confused, "Master Sparrow—why are you honouring us with your presence?" Now, naturally, silence descended. These might have been all new students, but they already knew how that title required at least a dozen years of studies. And that she addressed me, could sadly not have been more obvious.

I used Alexis' training in 'coping with situations' (especially those you don't want to be in, he had joked) and did a good impression of a smile. "I decided to study up on my angel 101," I replied politely.

The teacher smiled a little, very unsurely, "In that case, master Sparrow—welcome!"

I shook my head, "Master Sparrow is my brother." She smiled again, in a careful, maybe somewhat nervous fashion. Many years in the academic world had given me an exceptional knowledge of the rules. We ought to use first names, but I had the degree of master and she did not. So it was on me. "Call me Kiera," I decided.

"Christie," she replied with a slight nod.

She had turned to the blackboard, when she suddenly spun around again. "Kiera, you know what book we use?" it was only almost a question.

I nodded. "I've read it," I replied confidently.

"Already?" someone whispered behind me. I shrugged and just hoped that my behaviour made any kind of sense in this new not super academic world.

"Yes, I did so this morning." Christie was kind enough to let well enough alone and instead started to enlighten the others who were new.

At Another Time

Kiera watched Alexis work, fascinated. She had spent lots of time in his workshop during the last few weeks, but no one seemed to miss her. It wasn't very strange; her brother was constantly preoccupied with his studies.

Alex threaded the needle through the hand-sewn shirt one last time and smiled. "There." Han showed her the garment, a simple linen shirt with a silver buckle at the neck. "Now, it is as strong as armour," he explained. She peeked at it curiously from her place on the high chair.

"Does it have a name?" she wondered, full to the brim with curiosity as always.

"The shirt?" Alexis looked up in surprise.

She laughed at him. "No, the magic?"

"Oh. Yes, it is creator's magic. Crafting magic," the magician explained and started to pick out glowing pearls in all the colours of the rainbow, with every nuance Kiera could think of. "This is a discipline, an area," he simplified hastily, "which all who perform magical crafts are skilled in. It is fun, isn't it? Not quite as dusty as other magic," he added cheerfully.

"I want to become a magical crafter when I grow up!" Kiera decided in a very final way.

"I absolutely think so," the magician concurred and got out several thicknesses of the silver threads he seemingly used for practically everything.

"But you have to study for a long time to get to be one," the angel reminded her as he skilfully, almost casually, shaped the silver. "Do you want to study?"

Kiera squirmed. "My brother has talked about that I ought to learn stuff. Later," she shared reluctantly.

"Do you not want to, then?" Alexis glanced at the girl, who was now looking down into the table.

"My brother has started to show me things, sometimes. In the evenings," she looked even more miserable. "I don't understand much of it."

The magician patted her back. "Your brother is probably just bad at explaining. Academics can be like that." She shook her head, somewhat despondently.

"He shows me things in books…" Alexis, who was really rather a clever man, suddenly realised what was the matter.

"You cannot read?" he questioned carefully. She shook her head again.

"My parents didn't think it was important."

Alexis couldn't help a wide smile, simply from relief. "Don't you worry. That is easily fixed," he ruffled her hair as she looked up. "I will teach you. Don't you worry about that, *lilla sparv*."

Alexis had shaped the silver now. It was an exquisite little diadem of the type that circled the entire head. "What colours do you like the most?" the man asked the girl and quickly tried the basic shape in thread on her head. It fitted her perfectly. She attempted to trap his hands.

"What are you doing?" the eleven-year-old demanded to know.

The angel, who had given up keeping track of his own age many years ago, laughed at her irritation. "I am making a silver wreath for you, for the midsummer's feast," he replied and ruffled her hair again. "Your brother certainly won't." Something was hinted in his eyes, but he otherwise didn't let anything on, "Now, help me design it!"

They had gotten through extensive descriptions of the midsummer's traditions of at least ten separate cultures and had reached the point where Alexis was as giggly as Kiera, when the pretty little tiara was finished. Kiera, who obviously had quite good taste for one so young, had chosen several different nuances of blue to decorate with, and a lot of the silver still showed.

"Well, that turned out nicely," decided Alexis and looked down to the little tomboy at his left side. He gently put the crown on her head and asked permission to lift her down. They approached the mirror together.

The girl was quite small for her age, but the magician suspected that she would turn out quite tall with age. She was dressed in jeans, as indeed every time he had seen her, and a simple, blue tunic. He smiled crookedly to notice how determined her style already was.

The child's hair was as black as his own, but differently from his, which literally had barely seen a comb the last hundred years, it was tidily combed and fell in soft curls all the way down to her hips. A single golden streak, a flattering genetic mistake, broke the darkness. The crown in silver and blue fit the picture perfectly, matching her dark blue eyes. The magician was once more stuck by their similarity.

Even the girl, who did not think of such things in the same way, felt it natural and obvious how similar they were inside, but he was struck by how this similarity extended even to their physical appearance. He wished intensely that there might have been a reason for this, and finally had to smile at himself, while Kiera stood next to him and turned back and forth in her new silver and blue tiara. She really did awaken his paternal instincts, he couldn't deny it.

Alexis caught Kiera in a mischievous bear hug and peeked into the mirror with her. "So, are you satisfied?" he wondered. He was rewarded with an enthusiastic hug right back.

Back in Our Time

I awakened on Tuesday morning with the distinct feeling that something was off. Then I realised that all was silent, no stressed brother around or about, and looked at my clock. Half past three. I peeked out through the window, just to make sure it was not half an hour to four in the afternoon. It wasn't. It felt so surreal somehow. I had awakened by myself, just after three o'clock in the morning. Holy cricket. Naturally, going back asleep was impossible.

This was why, when my brother started to scramble about upstairs and came down the stairs around five am, I was sitting with my laptop in my lap, browsing YouTube for a video where the characters in *Lord of the rings* play truth or dare without Legolas turning out to secretly be gay. This was not an easy task.

I almost thought that Thomas would fall down the entire lower half of the staircase when he saw me sitting there. The absurd music coming from my computer might have been a contributing reason. Either way, it didn't help. But it did contribute to the crazy atmosphere.

"Good morning!" I greeted him cheerfully. "Slept well?" Thomas shook his head at me but replied politely that sure, he had.

"Did you sleep at all?" he wondered after that, while he hustled around looking for some book that he'd lost. Not strangely so, judging by how many books he had lying about the place.

"Sure," I replied, leaning back onto a huge pillow. "Several *hours'* worth of it." Something which could have been worry glimpsed in Thomas' quick glance in my direction. "You are not becoming ill, are you?" he questioned, and started to pack the now found book into his bag.

"Don't think so," I replied and smothered a sigh.

Though it happened that Thomas and I had a good time together, that he often took the time to teach me things and always did his best to be a parent for me, we weren't half as close as we could have been. I could remember no difference from when we were little. It had always been exciting when he got home from university, but I did not even remember the time when he had been living at home. We had probably never had any real contact with each other.

I gave the scientist, with the short, messy, brown hair a searching gaze. I very much liked my brother, but sometimes it felt like we had an ocean between us two. I gave him an indistinct wave goodbye when he said something absent-mindedly and walked towards the door.

When he was gone, I went and got a small pocket mirror with a frame of wood which he had given me as a child. My brother had brown eyes, fairly light. Mine were dark and blue. My brother had straight, short, brown hair moving through three adjacent nuances of colour. Mine was ebony black, curly and ended just above the hip. The colour was exactly the same without any differences, except a single golden lock. We really were not that similar, even on the outside. Had I not possessed facts to the contrary, I would have named Alexis, with his fire-blue eyes and his black hair, as my true brother.

I dumped myself down onto the carpet, just next to where I had left my computer. I had no lessons today, which meant that I had nothing to do, with all course literature read through. I had no workshop of my own, my book-based brother's workshop was useless for my work, and Alexis was very firm on never rising before eight am.

I suddenly realised that I was sulking. But was this what my life was going to be like from now on? Early mornings when I had nothing better to do than browse *YouTube*? No way! I was probably mid-through my most moping moment ever since age eight, when I realised something.

I wasn't just little Sparrow living with her brother any more, technically I hadn't been for some time, though some had still viewed me that way. Nor was I a student. I had my own master title and I was still studying... I rose and got out through the door at record speed. I was having breakfast early, because I had an errand to make.

Sonia at the University reception was happy to see me, as I turned up just as she opened up the reception at six. "Hi, *master* Sparrow!" she greeted me cheerfully, leaning over the counter to give me a hug. "Congratulations on the degree! *Degrees*!"

"Thank you," I smiled back, "it feels very strange."

"I can imagine that it does. What can I do for you today?"

"Since I took my master's degree, I am entitled to my own workshop, aren't I?" I questioned. She nodded, first surprised, then understanding.

"Starting to get old living with your brother, is it?" she wondered with a wide smile. I nodded again,

"Quite old. My brother and I have very little in common really," I shrugged. "In one way we are alike, we both live for our work, but we do have completely different directions on said work."

"Uhm," Sonia agreed, not looking up from the lists she had started to search through. "You know," she noted hopefully, "the little annex just by master Darn's large workshop is unoccupied. It isn't a place where most of us would choose to live," she looked up and smiled some, "mostly because we find him frightening. But it would be perfect for you, wouldn't it?"

When I nodded, she took the papers and the details for the flat out and placed them on the counter. We peeked at them together. It was perfect.

An hour later, Sonia's colleague had arrived and took over for a while, so that she could come with me to look at the apartment. We had dedicated the time up until then to paperwork.

The door, which was very old and special in a wonderful fashion, was an external door since the annex was added to the main building. It was more its own and more private than most of the university lodgings. Added to that fact was that the only other thing in that corridor was Alexis's living quarters and workshop, so most avoided it entirely. My heart beat fast as we unlocked the door and entered.

It was a pretty small room, but I liked it. Sonia saw my facial expression and laughed. "This is built at the same time, almost, as master Darn's annex next doors," she enlightened me, "that has an atria, too, right?" Oh, that was why it was so small. We went through a small, white wooden door of that kind that's wonderfully beautiful without even trying for it, and entered a large room with shelving around every wall except one big hole where a painting had probably hung long ago.

The room had two enormous windows with mullions and filled up the entire annex, except a balcony similar to the one in my brother's suite. A twisted staircase led up to it, and four pillars kept up the part of the inside balcony that wasn't resting on the rooms beneath it. We went into them and peeked.

There was only the one large room, entirely empty, underneath. The upstairs was different. One bedroom with huge windows and a fantastic bathroom, with a small dressing room between them. It was dusty and empty and in dire need of some paint, but it had wooden floors which would be fantastic after a thorough scrubbing, and I liked it already. This was cool. My own, my first fully my own, space. And considering the customs of the academic world, my residence for at least the upcoming 25 years.

Sonia had not joined me but stood a short distance away, examining the flaky paint on the walls of the great room. "I can send someone to paint it," she offered, but then gave me an amused look, "or I could simply leave it for a proper professional, master crafts-magician," she suggested.

"It is unusually lively in here," Alexis stood in the door, his lips curved by a smile. "Are you thinking about becoming my neighbour, lilla sparv?" he wondered. Sonia wished me luck and fled.

"Will you help me fix it up?" I asked Alex.

"Of course," he assured me. "Let's go to my workshop, I will have everything we need."

A lot can be said for creative magic; it is hard, time consuming to learn and few will be able to fully master it, even if they actually manage their graduation, which are pretty slim chances. All of those things are true, but if you take two people that *do* manage it: then things will move *fast*.

It was barely past eleven o'clock when I stood in my old bedroom and gathered my things into tidy boxes by way of magic. I had left Alexis standing in the middle of the large room, in the process of painting the walls in a perfect, sea blue colour. It made me happy just to look at it.

"Ready?" the magician suddenly stood in the doorway. I nodded and he cast a moving spell to bring what I had packed up. I did not master the required magic at quite such a level yet. "The place is all done, and yes, I remembered to clean out all the floors. Thoroughly," he predicted my question, "twice."

Eight o'clock in the evening, I was ready to go down to dinner. A lovely painting of a forest and a rope-bridge had surprised me as I returned from my luggage efforts; Alexis' housewarming present. Now I had unpacked, which was easy as I didn't have much stuff, and filled at least some space in the shelving with magical crafting tools and the approximately four dozen books I actually owned. I had fetched them where they stood accompanied by my brother's many books.

Alexis had helped me out with every large chore, which was why I had managed to settle my apartment in one day, but had left me with the details at about six o'clock. I suppose he thought I ought to get the chance to settle into my new home in peace.

Chapter 6

I was exhausted, both magically and physically, (and certainly physiologically) but certainly happy, when I filled a plate and sat down at Alexis' side. He was busy making neat little knots on his fork. That was rude of him, really.

At his other side, my brother was discussing the dangers of red magic with three of his colleagues, on his far side. I cut him off abruptly, something that always annoyed him. "What is so important?" Thomas questioned testily.

"I have moved into the small annex, in the dark corridor," I enlightened him neutrally. I answered his puzzled expression with calm. "I am not a pupil anymore, I need my own workshop. Anyway, I moved, just thought I'd let you know," I finished, and leant back in my chair.

My brother, who, all things considered, seemed to regain his ability to form words fairly promptly, had no chance at commenting. Alexis promptly started to discuss dream catchers with me, and whether I needed one work table or two. Or perhaps even more. And how did I want my atria decorated? He had painted it turquoise for me like I had asked him to, and placed the small white half-moon table that he no longer had any use for there, but it was still somewhat empty.

At Another Time

Kiera, still with the silver crown on her head, sat and looked on while Alexis made dream catchers, when someone knocked hard on the front door to his large workshop. That had never happened before. The workshop was located in a quiet part of the school, because there was nothing else in the dark corridor along with it. And Kiera had noticed that Alexis did not get many guests. Or, to be more specific, *any* guests, except herself.

Kiera remained in her high chair with her green chocolate cup while Alexis went out into the atria to open the front door. He closed the door between the rooms almost by reflex.

The Magician opened the door with a firm feeling that he'd rather not. It was the headmaster. Alexis raised an eyebrow, but he didn't comment. He didn't open the door wider for the man to enter, either, just awaited an explanation. The headmaster looked uncomfortable.

"Grandmaster Darn," he said by way of greeting, and tried a sort of downcast but pompous look as he spoke to the magician who was as powerful as a storm, but who didn't want to even touch much of what he could have been capable of. The angel did not even want to consider spending time with other academics! Or even be included in their number. (And he might have a point there, the ruler of the university privately noted tiredly.)

"Master Darn," the headmaster made another attempt. "A young girl has gotten lost. She is the sister of one of our younger, and very talented academics, and he cannot find her for supper," the headmaster shifted uncomfortably. "Can't you help us find her? One small search spell from you and we would find the child in…"

"No," Alexis cut him off, seemingly completely neutral. As ever. The headmaster sighed.

He was just about to give the magician a good talking to, despite the fact that he did not actually dare to, but despite it all he was worried something odd might be going on as children normally didn't get lost in his domain, and that had made him angry, when a scraping sound was heard from inside the magician's workshop. The headmaster did not find that strange, as he assumed that somebody spending so much time apart from everyone else as the angel did really ought to have a pet, but Alexis, who easily identified the sound and was afraid that Kiera would fall down from her chair if she wasn't careful, closed the door in the headmaster's face.

The magician met Kiera in the doorway between the atria and workshop. "You should have stayed seated," he chided carefully. "You could have hurt yourself."

"Who was it?" the child questioned curiously.

The angel sighed, "A boring academic. One day, you will be able to tell me yourself what in your opinion is the worst thing about living with all these academics," the magician prepared the child as they walked back into his study.

Back in Our Time

I had a gotten through a lesson about magical beings on Tuesday, and at the same time fallen in love with the practise of only rising two hours before my lectures began. I started to realise for myself why Alexis had his rule to only rise after eight. I couldn't remember to ever have done that before.

Tuesday afternoon, I spent with the study of angels, and yet another awkward moment appeared. Our guest teacher for the day had lectured a good while on how angels' wings worked, and then asked if we understood. I said no.

Our teacher gave me a questioning look. I forced myself to give an explanation. "I do not understand what you mean," I clarified, trying to sound as neutral as possible, "I do not agree that the process happens that way." Our guest lecturer, a male human of about 25 years of age whom I had never met before (most likely he was a guest from some other of the magical universities that was spread throughout the world) stared at me.

"I think my knowledge on the subject is somewhat more extensive than that of a beginner," he explained in a condescending tone. I noticed him carefully absorbing my looks. There were always idiots who curiously found this academically relevant. Mysterious.

"Is there some part in particular which you have trouble following, miss…"

"Master Sparrow," I corrected him. "Magician, actually. And I think not. My studies with Grandmaster Darn have given me quite extensive knowledge on the subject." I smiled innocently at him. There was nothing embarrassing about cutting short someone who was being rude, after all, and if he was rude I might as well return the favour.

"Why are you studying angels if you had the advantage of studying by *Darn*?" the lecturer's friend, who until now had remained in the background, wondered. Alexis name was well known in all academic and magical circuits. And in quite a few *not* so academic instances as well, for that matter.

"I wanted a break in my studies on magical beings," I replied nonchalantly. "I have foremost had angels and djinns around for so long that it was past the time to study them from a more formal viewpoint. But this is hardly the time for this conversation. If your friend might correct his facts, I think we would all like to continue this lecture." Our arrogant lecturer was pretty defeated at this point. It had been far too long since I got to tell somebody off. I had probably missed it, if I think about it more closely.

Before any of the youths (who were far older than I was) up by the blackboard had gotten themselves together, there was a knock on the lecture room door and two janitors appeared. "Excuse us," they said by way of greeting, and then one of them turned towards me. "Master Sparrow, since you have finished your basic studies and have your own workshop, could you turn over your workspace? We would need it for the new students."

"Oh sure," I had completely forgotten. "I can empty the room as soon as I am through here, so you can have it straight away tomorrow morning."

"We would actually need it quicker than that," the janitor who only now turned towards me admitted somewhat sheepishly. "Is it possible for you to deal with it before our workday is over?"

I frowned, "Maybe. I suppose I could go straight to deal with it and leave the rest of this lesson to fend for itself, I do not believe I am in danger of not being able to keep up."

"No need," Alexis, divinely well informed despite his habit of keeping to himself, had appeared in the open door. "I can take care of it."

"Okay. Could you place the furniture in my atria, please?" I asked, trying to recall where I had placed my spare key. The angel shook his head, "I will put them in mine, it isn't like there are many things. Or far to move them later. I'll be in my workshop when you're done here." I nodded, and he disappeared with the gracious, almost imperceptible movements which we humans could never quite mimic.

I turned to the janitors. "Alexis is quick," I told them. "You can probably go straight over." Our teacher and his friend were, after the sight of the both feared and respected magician, somewhat green in the face. Our lecturer called for a short break. Clever move. He definitely needed a moment to gather himself.

Quite a few of my, only somewhat older, course buddies gathered unexpectedly around me. "You call the magician Darn by his first name?" someone whispered.

"You have gotten your own master workshop?" someone else asked. I nodded somewhat, mostly to make them stop whispering over each other's words, and started explaining.

"I have known Alex, master Darn, since I was a kid. I lived with my brother, who is a master and specialist in 'transformation of the species', amongst other things, since I was eleven up until very recently, as I moved into my own apartment with a more suitable workshop."

"I never quite grasped that titles thing," someone admitted, a little bit sheepishly.

"What's what? You'd know, right?" Several faces nodded their agreement with the question.

"After six years you become a basic mage, then you get master at twelve and magician at thirteen," I summarised. I had learnt all about it long ago. "Three master titles are called a higher master, my brother is one, for example, and there is another level at the double, great master, but those two are human titles only, as we rarely have time to get to grandmaster, which is a full dozen of master titles."

"Like master Darn," someone wanted confirmed.

I laughed, "Well, in the sense that he passed all of those along the way. Alex is a Grand Magician, also called storm-master or storm-magician."

"That's what you are," I could not help becoming serious, "when you have power enough to summon storms, make lightning, when your magical power no longer can be measured. There has only ever been a handful. The only thing rarer is a master magician."

"And how do you become that?" the girl next to me asked curiously.

"You beat a grand magician at their own game," I grinned, "which includes almost anything at that point. It is the only title which is not strictly academic, even if you have to be a magician in the first place."

I paused before asking a question I was curious about. "You, who are students live in some sort of connected flats in connection to our workrooms, don't you? I have never been there, as I always stayed with my brother."

"We do," someone confirmed.

"What is it like, living with the magicians?" yet another person asked curiously.

I shrugged, "Academics are very special, but I am so very used to them. I find non-scholars far more difficult to understand, to be honest." I hesitated a little and then admitted, "Like, for example, when one of you complain that we get too much to read or research; in the academic world knowledge is the, well, driving force. Nobody is ever bothered by having to learn *too much.*"

"But is that never stressful then?" someone wondered.

I smiled, "Curiosity is many of the scientists' foremost quality. They do not do much beyond delving into their subject, so there's not that much stress after all, at the end of the day." I tried to put myself into the mind-set of my new friends and elaborated, "If you do not care to have time to even talk to people, just because you need to think for a while, or can happily drop everything to finish a book… then do you understand what it's like?" I added. "It is not a coincidence that most scientists and academics here have no partner or family, except some academics living with other academics, equally busy, or that kids are pretty rare."

We traded life experiences for a while longer and had a pretty good time, not to mention that the group grew as we went, but had to stop ourselves when the badly researched guest lecturer wanted to continue. But I had gotten an entire bunch of new friends, anyway.

I went in the direction of Alexis' workshop as soon as the lousy lecturer let us go. My new mates were forced to run off to one of the lectures on university rules which new students had to attend as soon as they arrived, so there was no point in staying to talk to anybody.

On the way over to the dark corridor, I ran into Alex and Robin. I seemed to have caught the 'sisters' in the middle of a conversation, but that apparently didn't bother them. "Hello, master!" Alex greeted me, while an expression I could not identify spread over the djinn's face. The downside with djinns was that they did not only ask less questions than angels did, they also gave fewer answers.

"Hi," I replied. "Where are you headed?"

Robin broke into the conversation, "The library. Pool. Where are you going?"

"Silly, she's on her way *home*," Alex cut in and smiled, "we heard that you got your own place now, entirely big-brother-free."

"That I don't know, Thomas knows where I live and besides, Alexis can be fairly much of one himself if needed," I retorted with a laugh, "but I am actually headed to visit my neighbour. Alexis, that is," I added.

"Have fun, and don't let him lose any feathers!" the siblings encouraged me, very djinn-ishly. And very strange, as they were the least djinn-ish djinns I knew. And I knew a *lot* of Djinns.

"Hello," Alexis answered absentmindedly as I entered his workshop, asking how his day was like. He was in the process of assembling an enormous number of pearls into a complex necklace, while they obediently floated around in the air before him, and was obviously very focused on getting it right.

I went to make some of Alexis's mysterious chocolate, which he had taught me how to make when I was a kid, and awaited him finishing up.

Twenty minutes later (only he could finish such a complex piece so quickly), we sat with our cocoa in the magical rope swing he had designed specially and hung up in the ceiling. I could remember a thousand occasions when he had made me hot chocolate as a child. Alexis was obviously of the opinion, and most kids would agree with him, that cocoa was a very important ingredient for children to be well. I am sure he was right.

Alexis had leaned his head back and looked up into the ceiling. Like all other space in his workshop, it was covered in first class crafts. The ceiling in particular was dominated by paintings, woodcuts, prints and mosaics.

"It has gone all the way around," I pointed out to him. He bent his neck back into a less painful-looking angle and gave me a questioning look. "You used to make this for me when I was small, now I am making it for you," I elaborated.

"It would only be a circle if I had become old and regressed to childhood," the angel pointed out, "your reasoning is far too human. You just grew up. That doesn't make a circle, it is a straight line."

He smiled a little, "It reminds me, however. When you were a little lass, I said once that when you'd grow up, you'd be able to tell me what you found to be the worst thing about being surrounded by academics. I have never asked you, but you ought to have formed an opinion by now," he grinned. "You've had plenty of time to think about it, not to mention a lot of experience by now."

I grinned back, "I remember," I replied. It was true. I could recall it perfectly. It was one of many nice, old memories I had of Alexis. Most of my oldest memories, and even more of my best childhood memories, included him.

"So, what is it? The far too constant environment?" Alex wondered, "I mean, even their motives are unmoving."

"No," I stated decidedly. I sighed.

"The worst thing about living amongst academics is when you wake up one day and realise that you've got a master title yourself. That you have a place beyond dispute at the academic's table, not just because they requested it, not anymore, but because that's where you belong. Then there simply isn't any cuss words that covers it!"

Alexis, who was the master of masters, or near enough, even held the almost impossible title of 'grand magician', chuckled at that, "I know the feeling, lilla sparv," he assured me. He rose, still chuckling, and put his cup down on a table nearby.

He took up a small bottle with a greenish liquid and started to carefully drop it down onto the small tomato plants which competed for the light with the large, strange plants living in a corner. Each plant grew a little bit and got new leaves from the liquid.

When he reached the last one, he dripped down just a little bit more of the magical plant food than he had for the others. It was impossible to discern if it had been on purpose or not, but the plant immediately grew half a metre high and tomatoes, both ripe and not, appeared on it.

"Oh dear, that one must have had a tad too much," he smilingly quoted the gall's effective, but doubtlessly slightly crazy druid Getafix. At least one thing was absolutely sure; Getafix-inspired, Skalman-loving Alexis, was quite a far cry from the organised academics. Not necessarily as far from the scientists, though, who were often pretty much insane too. And thank goodness they were.

At Another Time

Kiera had asked what seemed like a full million questions about everything between heaven and earth, delighted that the angel magician actually knew the type of things that she wanted to know, and Alexis had finished both the dream catcher he had been working on and yet another tiara, this one shaped into exquisite flowers, when he glanced at the clock.

"Oh my," he noted, ruffling the girl's hair. "The time is almost… do you know the clock, by the way?" he questioned

71

in passing. "It is past eight o'clock. We really ought to go join the dinner sitting."

"I thought that you ignored rules like that," the girl reminded him of his words from an earlier occasion.

"I do, quite right," he replied and reached his hands out for her. When she nodded, he easily lifted her down from the chair.

"But I have to stay orderly with you around, so I do not feed you a bunch of bad habits," he winked at her, "like adhering to rules…" When she laughed, he stated seriously, "Oh yes, that would be *bad*." Winking, he opened both doors for her and let her lead.

They were heading through the dark corridor when the magician questioned, "Do you want to go with me to dinner? You might not want your brother to see you with me? If he doesn't want you to be around me, he might scold you."

Kiera looked up at him in surprise. "How did you know?" she wondered seriously. How could Alex know what her brother said and thought?

"Your brother is an academic. We are at war!" the magician teased. "I am *dangerous*, too. Did no one tell you that?"

"Yes," the girl replied, frowning, "but you are so nice!"

The magician laughed, "I like you, little Kiera, so of course I am kind to you! Academics, on the other hand, who are always poking at everything and would prefer to examine both my magic powers and angels in general if they were only allowed. No thank you." He looked down to the girl, "There's no need for you to understand that. It is typical, weird, adult reasoning and had there been any sensible, slightly older people nearby, I would have told them instead."

Kiera looked back at him wisely, "You are here," she reminded him.

"That is right, but on the other hand, I am not as wise as you," the magician complimented her and bowed graciously for the child with the dark locks.

The girl laughed, "I think that you are really wise," she assured him, her voice carrying a critical undertone that made it perfectly clear that she knew some others of whom she did *not* have that opinion.

"So?" the magician reminded about a minute later, when they started to approach less forgotten parts of the university buildings, "do you want me to go another way?"

Kiera shook her head. "Why would someone not be allowed to talk to you," she demanded to know, but she wasn't actually asking him. "It is like some sort of *punishment*. And what did you do wrong?"

Alexis pondered this silently as they went. Kiera did not speak either. She still seemed upset on his part. It was a very strange experience for the powerful solitaire that someone defended him.

Well, what, quite, had he done? He continued to ponder. 'What hadn't he done' was maybe the more correct question. Volunteered as a test bunny, or helped to make experiments successful even though he easily could have; what with his knowledge of magic. Restrained his temper. Things he never had bothered to do.

Alexis did actually consider for a second if those were things he *should* have done, but he abandoned that train of thought. Controlled his temper, sure, maybe he should have done that at times when he had not, but except that he was who he was. He was ready to stand by that. When all is said and done, if not even someone with his strength could do that, what hope was there? And when it came to letting curious scientists poke at his abilities or ask nosey questions about his (lack of) wings: absolutely *not*!

The great magician and the magician-to-be continued their walk in silence. It was a bit of a walk from the dark corridor to the parts of the university buildings which were most actively used, but it was not a drastically long way to go. They did not encounter many people, and the ones they actually did meet tended to look away before even spotting Kiera. To bother storm-master Darn could only end badly. And since nobody knew what it took to be considered a bother, many decided to take no risks.

Alexis Darn stepped in through the dining hall's enormous doors with the kind of nonchalant self-confidence only shown by someone who nobody could put down. And also typical for somebody who got lots and lots of unwanted attention. Kiera walked next to him in a way typical for a child who gets too little attention; and too many rules, lectures and too much trouble.

The dining hall was louder than usual, and especially at the head tables there was a very lively discussion happening. It was impossible to hear what they said through the noise from the rest of the dining hall, but the headmaster, teachers and academics were arguing so intensely, no one even noticed Alexis, an occurrence most unusual indeed.

The magician used his magic, true to his habit, to get food both for himself and Kiera (as she was still somewhat too short to properly reach) and ruffled her hair while they went back towards the aisle. This was when someone finally did notice them.

The silence spread like paralysis in the hall when more and more people realised where to look. They first did not believe what they saw. Dark, stern master Darn walking with the small, just as dark girl beside him, having a, as far as they could tell, quiet but very interesting conversation. She looked up at him as if he was her guardian angel, or at least very close.

The only ones seemingly entirely unbothered by the sudden apparition were the academics at the high tables, as they were arguing as intensely as ever. "We do not have the resources to search the entire university for the girl, especially as Darn refuses to help!" was the headmaster's loud opinion.

"We cannot just leave her, she could be lost!" one voice objected.

"Make him change his mind," a scientist suggested.

"He threw the door shut in my face!" the headmaster objected.

"Where does the girl usually spend her time?" a teacher wondered, directing her question to Thomas Sparrow.

"I don't know, she is usually… well, just about at the university," the magician uttered vaguely and gestured with his hands offhandedly. Most of the hall was watching and waiting now.

"Kiera was exactly where she always is when you forget about her, Sparrow," Alex, who now had reached the table, stated sharply. "Sitting on top of a high chair in my workshop asking a thousand and one questions." Alex turned to the headmaster, the speechless academics and teachers surrounding him. "And *you* people, need to devote your searching skills some *serious* further work!"

Kiera was shyly heading for her place at the end of the academic head table. Her brother had insisted to keep her close, and that was as far as they were willing to oblige. "No," Alex stopped her, "come sit next to me. Eating with a flock of academics is boring enough, you do not have to sit with the very worst ones." He smiled. "Keep me company instead."

Alexis lifted Kiera up onto the chair at his left side, the place of the first lady. There hadn't been one in over a year. "You cannot lift me without asking first!" objected Kiera, just as decidedly as ever, never mind that it was the eleventh time. "This is a lady's place," she pointed out to him after he had sat down.

"Yes, but we have no one to sit there right now," he replied teasingly, "and if I occupy the place of honour, shouldn't that mean I get to choose one!"

"I am not a lady," the girl said soberly.

"Sure, you are," the magician objected with a wink. "Traditionally, to not to be one, means doing stupid adult things which you aren't adult nor stupid enough for yet, so surely you must be a lady, lilla sparv!"

The hall was still completely silent, at their end of it, anyway, but now Thomas Sparrow regained his ability to talk. "*Stay away* from my sister!" he threatened.

Alex just shook his head. "You are a terrible parent, and cannot even keep track of her," he noted politely.

"I am *teaching* her…" Thomas started, but Alexis cut him off sharply, his tone scornful.

"There's more than that to being a parent, and you can hardly even teach her all that much, judging by how many questions she is asking *me*!"

"I have been showing her…" started Thomas again, but Alex did not allow for him to continue this time either.

"You have been showing her things in books. Is she following, then? Has it even struck your mind that a child might need more time to study a page compared to what you do?" Kiera looked up at Alex worriedly, but there was no need. He said nothing about her secret reading problem, which he'd discovered about earlier that day.

Alex shook his head at the now silent Thomas. "Bad parent *and* bad teacher!" the magician sat down and magically snatched up Kiera's fork just as she was picking it up herself. "Alex!" she objected, to general surprise.

"Get it back then, go ahead, break the enchantment!" the magician encouraged her.

Several of the academics muttered at that, they thought it quite sadistic to ask a child such a thing, when not even masters in the trade could break his spells. Kiera did not see it that way. She stomped her foot, and seemingly used a sort of furious concentration, focused on the fork. It trembled. The upper part of the hall went silent yet again. The noise beginning to restart died once more.

"Good," Alex encouraged her, "a little bit more!" he turned to Thomas. "Know what, you go back to your studies and your research, and *I* will teach the girl what *she* likes to know." Without bothering to await a reply, or even provide the opportunity for one, the angel magician turned back to his friend and encouraged her as she got the fork to fall.

"Did you drop it?" she wondered. *Everyone* waited for the magician's reply.

"Nah," he replied lightly, "but I didn't use full force in the spell, either, not yet," he ruffled her hair yet again, "that'd be cheating. You are doing supremely well, lilla sparv." The girl smiled back. They started to discuss blue versus green magic while the dining hall slowly filled with noise again. Slightly shocked noise, this time. (It was not, in any way, the last.)

Back in Our Time

I went to dinner together with Alex, but we weren't talking. We had just had a several hour's long discussion which would have been enough to give a 'real' academic a headache, and I at least needed time to reorganise inside my head. I couldn't tell if Alexis was doing the same, stayed silent because he could sense I obviously badly needed it, or indeed was pondering something else entirely already. Djinns might have been the masters of mystery, but angels can be ever so difficult to read, as well.

I met Thomas in the line. "Hi, little sister," he greeted me somewhat doubtfully.

I smiled in return, "Good evening, Thomas."

My brother exhibited a rare flair of temper. "Stop ignoring me. What is it *with* you and breaking the rules?"

I grinned as Alexis, the crownless king of breaking unwritten, academic customs, joined the ranks, so to speak, appearing at my side. Not to mention how my friendship with him was the first large upset I had ever caused to my brother's tidy system. And I think neither of them had forgotten. *Especially* not Thomas.

Thomas was just about to elaborate his part of the conversation (which we didn't strictly have) into a proper dressing down as I turned towards him and decidedly, although politely, explained; "Thomas. You stepped up as a parent for me after Mum and Dad, but now I am reaching on eighteen years old and have a degree as a full magician. I can write my own goals and live after my own rulebook. Got it? Just accept it, drop it, and move on!"

For a moment, Thomas was completely silent. Then he nodded, neutral enough to almost match Alex, before smiling weakly. "All right, little sister. All right," he replied, and walked off with his plate.

"Hmmm. A *showdown* with a happy ending," Alexis stated and nonchalantly waved some food onto his plate by magic, "fancy that." I gave my sarcastic best friend a, not entirely gentle, nudge.

Chapter 7

Thursday morning, I turned up for my next lesson on magical beings. It felt weird to be back beside super academic basic mages ten years my elder. I liked it by my age equals, after a little practise.

We were quickly informed that today's lessons would be on the subject of angels. Their culture, nature, physics and the very few diseases which could affect them. The first forty-five minutes of the lecture was spent on how their muscles differentiated from those of djinns and of humans, which probably was the least complicated part of the subject, then we got to the disease part.

"Anybody who can give any suggestions on any diseases which angels can suffer from?" the professor asked.

I raised my hand. "There are really only three, unless you count cataracts, which happens to elder angels sometimes," I replied.

"Right so far," he granted. "And what illnesses are these? Well, two genetic defects, based in their wings, one of them tremendously serious, and one type of flu which they can catch."

"Angel fever!" I remembered. "Or 'Angel's Plague'. Magic won't touch it, but there's plenty of herbs that will help."

"Exactly right. Well, angels suffering from cataracts are treated just like we in magic circles treat it in humans, a spot of directed healing magic and the problem is solved. It does happen that it recurs after a few hundred years, but as the treatment is so simple, this is not generally considered a problem. Many angels can even treat themselves. Though there tends to be a certain amount of teasing from other angels displayed towards those affected." No kidding. I had heard Alex talk of it. Apparently, it was considered hilariously funny.

"'Angel's Plague'," our lecturer continued, "is a form of magic resistant, severe flu as far as essentials go, and is the only disease which angels can actually catch. It does not infect creatures whose being isn't magic, like humans, which is why humans often treat it, but Djinns die from it regularly.

"Angels actually do rather well with it, it is mostly harmful to Djinns, as I said, but the name comes from that it actually *can* infect angels, which nothing else does. The latter is one of the reasons why angels make such fantastic healers. Another is, of course, the width and strength of their magic force.

"Affected angels are rarely sick enough for their lives to be in danger, and only two deaths have ever been recorded. Usually, it will be like an ordinary human flu, or only a mild cold, if the angel is very powerful." The lecturer turned to me, "Out of pure curiosity, master Sparrow, do you know if our storm-master Darn ever has been affected?"

I considered the answer, but decided that it wouldn't be to expose Alex. He was so careful about keeping his personal life private. "There are enough djinns here to make it surface from time to time, as I am sure you know," two djinns had died from it just a few years earlier in the infirmary, so probably they did. "Alexis caught it one time, and ended up sneezing for approximately three days. Afterwards, he said he pitied me for being human and catching colds," I smiled at remembering that.

It got somewhat more interesting as we got to the two genetic conditions of the angels'; K'siri and Evara. "K'siri is a dominant genetic mutation and can for this reason easily be followed through the relevant family trees," our lecturer enlightened us, "its effect is that the affected angel's wings no longer remain white, but are coloured. Depending on the exact protein it blocks in specific families, they receive different colours. Known today is the orange-red wings of many of the members of one of their oldest families, and also blue, grey and brown wings. We also know of an individual who, due to a personal mutation, had wings which became black.

"K'siri is usually counted amongst the very few diseases that angels can be struck by, but is in reality a completely harmless, often even appreciated mutation. Most angels carrying these genes like their wings exactly as they are. The alternative exists to with magic, more permanently or merely for a time, dye the wings white. It is not hard to do so, but very unusual."

The man up by the blackboard paused, for a brief moment. "The last disease, Evara, is neither easily cured, passing or a harmless colour change. It is singlehandedly one of the most usual reasons, next to accidents, including magic ones, for the death of an angel." He made it sound like an angel dying was a normal occurrence. It wasn't. They rarely sustained bad injuries in accidents, did not age and did not even share in the peculiar human habit of killing each other off very often.

The lecturer continued. "It is a recessive genetic condition which means that the affected angel's wings very painfully and slowly breaks down, until they are helplessly ruined and the disease instead eats the angel in question from inside. There is no known cure." He looked personally affected by this sad fact. Maybe he was.

"Already at birth, the wings are too badly injured to ever carry the angel in flight, and the pain starts in childhood. The illness usually starts to spread in their bodies age 200–400, depending on yet undetermined variables, maybe satisfactory research on the subject will come down to someone in here. Death usually occurs during their eight century, age 700–800. It happens that they live longer, especially powerful magicians, but no one has ever reached millennium age who has suffered from this terrible illness.

Being a recessive ailment, it usually comes as a surprise as many generations might have passed on both sides of the family since anyone last had a partner with the same defect gene, and the illness thereby has gone unnoticed." We were all of us rather solemn as we headed for lunch, and I hoped that the afternoon's go-through of the angel's culture would be somewhat less bleak.

It was, actually, not to mention that Alex, who didn't know about the subject of my morning lecture, held a considerably more cheerful lecture about the feathers of angels and birds during lunch.

Once it was time for dinner I had only just managed to drop off my notes and attempt to process the most overwhelming parts of the new information. The latter was, at the end of the day, not really all that difficult. I might not, at my heart and soul, be a proper academic, but I can obviously get a masters rank in half the time it takes them to do it. I believe the word is 'touché'.

I went to the hall for dinner, only to, to my joy, discover that they served pancakes. I had filled up my plate and was headed up to the head tables, when I glanced behind me and noticed that the generally pretty empty notice board made by oak (and how very impractical *that* is) which had last week enlightened everybody as to who had just made master or magician, announced a new set of news.

More specifically, it announced that 'only seventeen years old master Kiera Sparrow' from the 'at the university esteemed' family Sparrow had been awarded an official seat at the head table of 'the scientists, the magicians and the academics'. I had even been presented as their first lady! This because of my early degree and 'magnificent work and skill within her own field, crafts-magic'.

I stared at the paper for half a second after I had stopped reading, turned around and started to walk again, with the distinct difference that I now had to strain myself not to run. All honour to honours, but I'd prefer to just be left in peace, please!

I had just sat down, when Alex appeared beside me and sat down too. "Look at that, you're sitting in *your* place!" the magician announced with a teasing smile. He received my murderous glare with supreme calm. "I know the feeling. Sometimes, 'recognition' is the last thing you want."

I shrugged. "Why would a bunch of academics choose to place two anti-academics in honorary spots?"

I got a shrug back. "Because we're the best at what we do."

"There must be someone better than me within some of all the other fields somewhere," I pointed out. "I am aware that I am good within the field of crafting magic, no wonder after all the tricky techniques and spells you taught me as a child, but…"

"You graduated quicker than any of them," Alexis replied nonchalantly and put jam onto his pancakes, "you are appropriate for the position, many of your friends carry great power around here, which means more than you'd think. All in all, you're a comfortable candidate, and still worthy. It isn't strange at all."

Before I could get my own back to Alexis, we were interrupted by a loud bang. It was not a natural kind of bang. Experiments could sometimes end in a lot of noise, never mind if that was the actual intention or not, but this was not the case now. It wasn't a dropped plate or a glass reduced to a thousand pieces, either. One of the stately pillars of the hall had fallen straight across the mid-hall path. The markings, and the magical traces on the base of the pillar, were clear even from a distance. Somebody had caused it to fall.

Silence reigned for three seconds. Then someone started screaming, and the level of noise rose rapidly. The noise when everybody tried to leave was raised further when the tables were lifted. They flew to the side and hit the walls with a bang.

That would have taken some fairly impressive magic, but there were no visible traces left behind by it. I turned my head to look at Alex, whose dark eyes revealed that he was the one trying to help people to get out.

But those trying to leave the hall were hindered at the door. A magical barrage, composed by many colours and even more magical sources, slid into place and blocked it off as a number of humans, djinns and even an angel entered.

It was the djinns Robin and Alex, several of the human academics residing at the university and Irria, one of only three angels in residence at the university (and one was presently in Sweden examining alpine mosses. It was fairly common for *him*).

Irria was the one to speak. "We thought to make a few changes around here," she made clear. "First and foremost, the leaders will now be angels, of course! Everybody knows we are far more powerful compared to the rest of you, so why not use some *logic*." Alex's facial expression clearly told me that whatever *logic* she was using, he did *not* subscribe to the same kind.

"Secondly, the djinns are next."

"Sure, being a human is just so *lame*!" I responded, loud and clear. Despite it all, I am not a meek little girl with braids and no voice, and this was bound to end in a violent fashion anyway.

"To be an angel feels pretty silly too right now," Alex noted next to me.

"Alexis," Irria started.

The magician's expression was fantastic, "No please," he asked, "don't do the dramatic 'you ought to be on our side' monologue!" his laughter was likely the most provocative move he could have made. Just as well. Some things aren't meant to be delayed.

"Alexis, you managed to stop our last attempt, but this time it isn't worth your effort to try. That was just *humans* after all!" Irria's voice was soft and condescending. Then she turned to the rest of the hall and changed her tone. "Either you will accept the new order, or you can try to fight your way past us!" the young angel invited.

"Or, let's look to the fact that your little coup has been entirely useless until now, that," I judged their number; they weren't that many, "a fifth of you are already locked up tightly… then we might add your insanity to the odds. Is that to your detriment or advantage, you'd say?"

"Now, wait a second," the headmaster cut through the tirade authoritatively. "You cannot just…" Irria raised a hand and sent out a shock wave of magic that surely would have killed him, had it not on the way been intercepted by something considerably more powerful. Alex, too, had raised his hand, and now he jumped elegantly over the head table, (one out of merely two tables that he hadn't already gotten rid of) and walked through the hall.

"This is the *opportunity*," Alexis started while Irria's visible magic bounced against the invisible shield that apparently surrounded him, if he actually needed one. "The opportunity for me to give you *one final chance* at surrender. Then, most unexpectedly, you will suddenly grow a sense of moral, beg for mercy, run off and grow flowers in the holy land with a bunch of fluffy bunnies." The elder angel offered as education with his deep, firmly set voice.

"But that's not how I work. Either I've got you now, or you'll have to fight me." His smile was now not only fierce, it was frightening. The djinns, Alex and Robin, went into a magic-performing pose with their hands linked behind Irria. I raised an eyebrow. Was the plan *actually* to *fight Alexis*? Were they *entirely STUPID*?

There were just fifteen metres between them now. I had followed Alex, like most others seated with us, and we had come to stand in an uneven circle around them, about 20 metres away. Irria and her followers had left the door with its magical stop and were standing right in front of Alex, who was standing in the middle of the hall, all alone.

Alex and Robin were, if I was anyone to judge, a most excellent backup, and Irria stood her ground fairly nicely, even though her hair and shimmering blue wings were glowing with the effort. Then we all realised why. *She* attacked *him*. All her opponent did was to draw in the magic, using it to pull more magic out of her, drying it up faster than she could calculate.

This was when the magicians behind her started to fell pillars. The surrounding magicians used their own spells to offset the original castings or to protect themselves and the not-so-magical people around them. I felt my heart pounding. The air was full of the skimmer of magic from all the spells casted by everyone except Alexis, and the air smelled of salt from the sweat of all these people straining themselves, on both sides.

The sound of stone cracking, breaking and falling drowned out screaming and attempts at cooperation by oral means. Lanterns with candles fell and the usual light was partly replaced by the glittering of magic colours. As the seconds passed, the stones stopped falling. The magicians outside of the little rebel group might have been unprepared, but there were more of them. (And, I suspect, they were rather better, too.) If it weren't for the absence of most of the djinns (they had little need to eat as often as humans, hence few of them attended dinner) maybe a battle had not even been necessary, outside of the angel duel.

But there was a battle, right here, and now. And even though I could guess as to what the outcome would be, my hands were shaking with the adrenaline. The magicians could stop a whole lot of pillars from falling, but what about those that did fall? How long before they fell over somebody? What was I going to *do*?

Irria now sent an increasing amount of missiles, all of different colours of magic, against her older, and considerably more powerful, opponent, with the help of her company of djinns, and people. She was tired, but far from over. Then Alex sent his first, and as it turned out; only, attack.

What types of magic were contained in that spell, most may never know, but the visible form was that of crimson phoenixes. In a second, they pierced Irria's attacks, then they pierced her.

The second after Alexis' display, all was silent. Then came her chilling scream, and she seemed to break into pieces internally, even though there was no blood on the outside, no classic outer signs of any injury, and a couple of seconds later she fell down onto the floor, yet screaming. Before the djinns could reach her, (and they were yet only two steps away from her), she was silent.

A handful of powerful magicians, my brother included, immediately overpowered the human magicians the angel had brought. This was when the ceiling started to crack out of the pure force of the magic beneath it, and because of all the pillars that had fallen.

The rest of the djinns at University, who of course had felt the duel in every fibre of their bodies (they weren't magical beings for nothing) broke through the magic wall at the doorway seconds later and took on what they themselves considered *their* own task. Alex and Robin.

I watched in shock as two of my friends, as far as I knew, were overrun and screamed. The rest of the magicians and masters in the hall did their best to stop the cracks in the ceiling from spreading, or the pillars from collapsing. But it was clear they were losing that battle.

I instinctively looked for my friends and my family, to see where they were. Were they all right? Were they *alive*? What if someone had gotten hit by a pillar! Dhrar and Charl (who did not seem even a bit unsteady at the moment, but very powerful and *pissed off*) were helping to seal Robin into a secure cocoon of power that would be inescapable. My brother stood facing a pillar, holding it up with a multi-coloured shimmer of magic. At least it hadn't fallen over him. Yet. Alex. Alex wasn't where I'd last seen him.

Alex was kneeling in the centre of the room, face down and his hands raised. His palms were turned up as he turned to the ancient forms of magic which were *sung*. His voice was a faultless soprano, clear and perfect. There was a clarity to it rarely heard. The nearest I could think of was the type of voice certain small, human boys had before puberty.

All stood still and stared, listening, from the first note, but I only felt a second of temptation to join them. I might have stood like petrified up until now, for the very simple reason that I did not know what else I should have *done*, but everything has its time. Combat magic has its time and knowledge has its. Art has its time and crafts-magic has *its*. I ran up and knelt next to him, braided my blue magic and my alto voice together with his.

I allowed my, considerably smaller, magical power flow together with the angel's and Alex grasped my hand for a moment, before he once more turned the palm of his hand upwards. I felt the weight of our spell. The sheer enormous *force* it took to keep the ceiling up, despite all the help we got with that, and healing every crack, compensate for every fall. Stone needed to be lifted *back up* and to be joined together once more.

Luckily, Alexis provided most of the power behind our spell, which was doing most of the work even though every magician in the hall contributed in some way. Even the headmaster, who had not even gotten up, was surrounded by an orange cloud of magic.

The spell suddenly lightened its pressure as the djinns joined in. But it was up to Alex to join together the seams of the ceiling. Not even I could help him there. I backed away from the spell, letting him finish on his own, and fell down onto the floor. I felt a pressure over my collarbone.

His head raised still, the palms of his hands directed to his craft and surrounded by magic so powerful that the air was glimmering even from his colourless efforts, and he kept his focus perfectly. He did not miss one note in the ancient magical songs, and his pure, silver crisp soprano could be heard perfectly even through the noise the stone made. And then everything was silent except for the last tones of his voice.

All the pillars stood just as they had done before. The ceiling was whole, smooth and perfect. The words of wisdom written in it, in between the pillars, didn't lack one single letter. The creating magic had recreated everything as it had been and ought to be, and the spell had been perfected.

Alex got up as his last note had faded. He groaned somewhat as he stretched, and allowed a small sliver of healing, for once visible, purple magic fade into his stiff neck. Then he looked down to me, as I was lying four steps away from him, and his eyes went from magical to worried. Then they shifted just as quickly again, back to the dark colour, filled with magic.

He more or less floated towards me, so fast and soft were his steps, and knelt for the second time. I felt the angel gather his magic to him again. And I heard my brother come running, shouting. His steps were not half as silent nor half as elegant as those of the other magician.

"How is the girl?" someone else wondered. Other voices asked the same.

"Is she alive?" and, "dear, how did she do?" other voices were whispering, interspersed with concern for others who were not on their feet after the battle, further away from us.

"She has two broken bones. The Averisc magic was simply far too strong for her body," Alex enlightened us calmly. I felt him join my bones together again, but no pain. Probably his doing, but it could just as well be adrenaline at this point.

"How could you expose her to that magic?" Thomas raged. "You could have *killed* her!"

"Oh come on, do you really think I haven't used Averisc magic before?" I questioned tiredly. Silence descended completely yet again, at least in our little bubble. For once, people at a distance were too busy to be concerned with us at all.

"It is dangerous!" my brother burst out.

"Yes, because I would *certainly* have let her kill herself by accident," Alex answered, his tone lightly ironic. "Not all that likely."

"It is very useful within much of crafting magic," I informed my brother, allowing the magician to help me stand as I got up. My bones were whole, but I was exhausted.

Thomas embraced me before I had properly gotten my breath back. "I chose to expose myself to that charm," I assured him. "I am a crafts-magician myself, remember? I was well aware what Alex was doing before I got into it, and I knew I could help out." I stretched carefully as Alex got Thomas to lighten up his grip a little bit, and they both supported me.

"Besides, I'm okay," I finished. Then I frowned, "Well, I've got no broken bones. I will be fine after some sleep and a way to cure my upcoming muscle soreness, which I am sure I am due for tomorrow."

"We can fix that," Alex grinned. Quite a few conversations of the moderated kind, and a couple of the very official, followed this. A couple of magicians, like my brother, cooperated with the djinns to put all the tables back in order, and yet a few others cleaned up the mess resulting from all of this, and somehow it ended up with everyone having dinner yet again. This time joined by the djinns, though most of them were just ranting.

I sat leaning against a stone pillar and watched everyone be surprised about how Alex had saved the day, and laughed carefully (my entire body was still somewhat sore) at his, "What, just because I am unconventional and somewhat badly tempered, I cannot *help*?" explanation. I was actually not the only one.

Even though I was sore throughout my body, there was one source of sharper pain. One of my broken bones, something down in the leg, did not hurt at all, but my collarbone ached. I pulled at the fabric of my green tunic and looked at it. The tattoo of a broken feather that I carried just across my right collarbone was glowing.

I did not need to ask anyone to know what that meant. The powerful magic spells Alexis had woven into it to protect me had taken effect on their own, just like they were meant to do if I was ever in danger, and had protected me from some of the pure force of the spell I had gotten myself into. In fact, the very bone underneath it had broken from the raw strength of the energy that was absorbed and released there. That my ribs were whole was a miracle, but the bespelled tattoo had done what it was supposed to do. I had gotten just a little bit of help when I needed it the most.

While I hid my tattoo before someone started asking questions (I really did not need to have to try and *think*), it started to seep out of the whispered conversations that most people actually hadn't known exactly *how* powerful Alexis really was. Now, in the light of what had just happened, it grew painfully obvious quite how much damage he could have done had it been him starting a crazy rebel coup. This reasoning might have brought with it more than a little panic, before the insight that he had actually never done anything like it, not in all this time, sank in and mixed with the knowledge of what he *had* just done.

In the end, I think Alexis became even more of a mystery than ever, but despite that, I think most understood him just a little bit better than before. If nothing else they had all had a glimpse of my friend, the man I saw when looking at him. A protective, loyal magician who *sang* and never got cocky, no matter what he pulled off. True, false modesty wasn't a main feature of his (but who likes that anyway, honestly?), but he never bragged. About anything. And he *really* could have.

As matters started to calm down, even on the mental and administrative levels, and the crooks were safely contained, I sat up at the head table and had more pancakes. My brother had carried me there, because I didn't manage to walk yet on my newly healed leg.

Alexis and the djinns had been gone for a while by then, since they had disappeared off to construct a magical prison inside the ancient cells of the school. Judging by the joint magical force they commanded no one would ever be able to break out, or in, of that place *ever again*.

To improve the matter even further, Alexis had permanently stolen the magic of the human magicians, and the djinns had made sure Alex (the djinn) as well as Robin wouldn't be able to as much as lift a pencil with theirs for many, many years.

I had just started to nod off with my head against the back of my chair, when Alex (the angel version) came and lifted me up. "You are not allowed to lift me without asking for permission," I objected, just as I always had done when I was a child.

Only this time, it was so much more devoid of power. Alexis though sounded exactly like he always had when he replied, "Forgive me, lilla sparv."

The magician obviously said a couple of calming words to my brother, which he apparently accepted, but I did not hear them. Alexis carried me, with an angel's effortless strength, away from the dining hall.

Chapter 8

I collapsed into Alexis' rope swing and closed my eyes. "Wow, somebody's been using *awesome* magic!" the angel magician joked. He sat down beside me and eased a cup of cocoa into one of my hands, "being tired is normal, lilla sparv."

I forced my eyes open to look at him. "What about you? Aren't you the least bit tired?" I questioned, my tone sceptic.

He laughed. "I do feel in my muscles that I really worked hard, yes, but it is just like your running." He smiled again, "Working out is nice. Speaking of that, why haven't you been running ever since you got your degree?"

I moaned, "Too much new! I will run, but not today, and certainly not tomorrow." Alexis laughed again, and gave me a soft nudge to make me drink my chocolate.

"Speaking of mystery, which we weren't," I suddenly remembered something which had appeared in my head much earlier that day, before all of this mess started. "Why did you *really* cut your wings? And why aren't they growing back out by now? I know very well that they do so on more powerful angels," I grinned, but didn't bother to keep my eyes open, "and don't even try to sell to me that that doesn't include you. I'm not buying it."

Alexis hesitated. I could feel it clearly. I snapped my eyes open so that I could catch his gaze. "After all this time, don't you think that you could trust me enough to tell me? I do not even know how many times my life, oh, I know it very well, in our experiments, and this very night, have been in your hands entirely. But you don't want to give up your secret? *Alex*!"

Alexis gave me a smile, and reached out a hand to close my eyes again.

"I am very used to not mentioning certain things out loud," he started, "that's why I've never told you, not lack of trust. I trust you, just like you can always trust me."

He was silent for a short while and then continued, "I was always a skilled magician, far before I took any degrees. Before there *were* any degrees which I could take." I could hear him smiling, "That's a side effect of being monumentally old. In any case, magic was always my forte.

"Already as a child I could fly by way of it, I still can, as I am sure you have seen if I have needed to get stuff from far up," I nodded in confirmation. Sure I knew. I had seen him do so since I was a child, par the usual.

"Exactly," the magician continued. "But what other angels did, when they were carried on the wind itself by their wings, I couldn't do it." Horror made me open my eyes. Despite his voice being neutral, the sorrow was obvious. And I knew him so well…

"My wings never worked like they were meant to," he continued, "and I was not old at all when they started to hurt."

"Oh!" I commented involuntarily as I suddenly understood. My studies had, in a way, prepared me for this. "You had one of the diseases angels can get in their wings!" Alexis nodded, and at this point I was staring at him, tiredness; poof.

"Yes, exactly," the angel confirmed sadly, "so I used my magic to… well, really to cut everything out that makes wings work and grow, actually. It is impossible to get rid of all those traces, not even I can change the physiology of an angel to that extent, and so that's why my feathers still grow sometimes. But the wings are gone, and so is the pain." He gave a sudden laugh, the saddest laughter, not to mention sound, I had ever heard, and noted, "I am quite literally depraved, like they say, only not mentally. But without wings, the disease had nothing in which to grow, so it never spread to the rest of me."

He was silent for a short second and then, "I have searched more closely with magic since then. The sickness is gone, I actually managed to get rid of it, but as a bargain, my wings are beyond any and all help in return."

"But they would still be unusable, wouldn't they," I noted silently, "that is how it works. It is a genetic flaw, which starts in the wings and spreads through the centuries until it kills the angel, isn't that so?" The nod was a confirmation.

"One of the few things I really mourn is that I never got the opportunity to feel what it is like; to be carried by your wings," admitted Alexis. "No matter how it might seem, I am fairly happy as things stand, but that is like a hole going right through me. What I do is not the same." I understood. Angels had a longing to fly, to get to use their wings, and Alex couldn't do it. I could, vaguely and dimly, discern what I would have felt like, having had my legs cut off. To never run again…

"Ah well; it is only one thing. There are many important things here in this world." Alexis comforted himself and gave me a soft nudge. "Friendship, crafts, *teasing academics*! Don't you agree, lilla sparv?"

I nodded and leant my head against his chest, my beloved adoptive brother and best friend, and fell asleep. I only half noticed how he saved my cup of cocoa from a certain death.

At Another Time

The dining hall was adorned with flowers. Wreaths, garlands, vases and pots. Academics have a tendency to be rather intense, and you could tell from all the ideas they'd come up with. The hall was splendid. Thomas Sparrow sat with a group of academics and discussed the many symbols of this festival, and it was difficult to say if he had chosen not to notice his sister when she had so obviously disregarded his rules, or if he had simply forgot about her for the moment.

The hall was quickly, but peacefully, filled by laughter, jokes, and people (amongst others) in colourful clothes. Every woman beneath the age of forty had flowers of some type in their hair, and many of the older ones too. Some men had defied prejudice and wore flowers, as well.

The few children who lived at university either acted like little models of their parents or like physical representations of any prejudice ever known about female and male. (Granted, not all of them *were* actually of the sex they represented in this prejudice, but then again they never are.) The thoroughly academic children sat at a long table and had a supremely serious discussion about why you ought to be given midsummer presents just like Christmas ones.

The boys, and two of the girls, hunted each other around the hall with the pillars as a hindrance to play around, and four little girls stood whispering together like only little girls can. Not even teenage girls do it quite as well.

One child stood out from the other, flowered little ones. Kiera Sparrow was leaning against a pillar, looking far ahead. Almost everyone, the only exceptions a couple of slightly too focused beings, noticed her.

The girl was wearing jeans, and a dark blue tunic with a ton of small silver flowers at the hem. She was the only child who wasn't wearing any live flowers. An exquisite silver diadem, the quality of which clearly identified who was behind the craftsmanship, adorned her hair instead of a flower garland.

Kiera pondered last year's summer, at home with her mother and father. She had noticed that she recalled them all the more rarely of late, as young as she was, but perhaps just because of it, she felt little guilt about this.

Or it was the fact that she knew how they had left her, and why they had done so. It had not been an accident, illness or any of those matters which, if they existed, could be said to be worth dying for. It was a silly argument. It had only been about winning.

The girl had decided that it was all very tragic, but not her fault nor in her power to change, when the doors opened. Just like every midsummer, when the enormous, stately oak doors into the hall were for once not wide open, Alexis Darn made a grand, double door entrance.

He had not replaced his jeans, but that was the only thing he hadn't done. The magician wore a richly embroidered, magnificent black cape, open at the front and lined with a silk fabric the exact shade of his eyes. Beneath it, he had a soft silk shirt with white pearl embroideries. He had matched the clothes with soft, black leather boots and blue metal flowers which were climbing from the neck of his cape up into his hair. He literally looked angelic.

The magician looked out across the room at everybody who had turned around to look at him, and the searching gaze he for long moments directed at them made him look even grander. It took him half a minute to spot Kiera. When he did, he turned to her and smiled.

Kiera smiled back, forgetting last year with her parents, who had not celebrated midsummer. The girl ran to meet the magician and laughed as he lifted her up, spinning several full circles. "Now we shall have a glad, and fun, midsummer's solstice, lilla sparv!" he determined, where after he lightly pointed out, while he put her back down again, "you know, we match!"

Back in Our Time

I was woken up by the pre-noon light beaming in through one of the windows in Alexis' workshop. The angel sat high up in an empty spot on top of one of his bookcases, and was picking leaves from one of his mysterious plants. He peeked down onto his tomatoes, which were growing in the same corner. I felt about as if I had been driven over, or exercised for perhaps half a year without pausing, judging by the soreness in my muscles.

Alexis, who naturally had noticed that I had awakened, pointed to the table in front of me. There was a big, brown cup placed on it. "Drink that. It should take the edge off the pain." He turned his attention back to his plants, but he continued to talk. "Only not all pain. You have to remember what your body has been through, or else you will strain the muscles once more. I think we will hold off using more healing at this point."

"How could the djinns steal Alex and Robin's magic for such a long time?" I wondered as I reached for my cup. Reaching over to the table hurt, but I assumed it would get better momentarily. "Not even you can do that."

Alexis chuckled. "There are things others can do which I cannot," he noted, "as you learnt last night," he grinned, apparently not about to let on the pain in what he had told me about his wings. "About that skill in particular though, as a matter of fact, I can, even if it is supremely hard, not to mention harsh, to do so quite as permanently as the spell yesterday, when it concerns magical beings. That didn't stop Charl though. Hir is actually the foremost expert on djinn magic now living in the entire world."

"*Charl*? A great magician? *Any* kind of magician?" I questioned incredulously as I tasted the content of the cup. It tasted exactly as Alexis' chocolate always tasted. Though I really should have seen that one coming. The angel magician did not share the viewpoint that medicine, or magical brews, needed to taste terrible.

"Yes, actually. Grand magician, even, to be perfectly frank with you. Charl is one of the greats," Alexis replied completely unmoved by my disbelief and took a magically slowed step down from the plants. "But djinn magic is not like other magic. We learn to channel the magic within ourselves, and control the power from outside. The djinns, on the other hand, are mere vessels for their magic. They can control it, yes, but too large amounts are dangerous to the djinns themselves. Charl can control it, yes, but it has not been good for hir mind."

I sipped my magical healing chocolate silently.

"It is a pity," Alexis continued sadly, "we used to have quite interesting discussions, many centuries past. Now hir spends time with djinns who, relatively speaking, are your age and everyone assumes that hir is one of them. But at times like yesterday, then we get a mere glimpse of who Charl really is. *What* hir really is. Or was, at least, at any rate."

"Wouldn't it be possible to help Charl using some type of magic?" I asked.

Alexis shrugged somewhat, "Perhaps. Not with traditional magic, but you who are young and foolish should maybe give it a try. Crafting magic could perhaps create some kind of aiding formula for hir. But if you are getting into such matters you have to understand one thing, if in case." Alexis came and sat at the edge of the seat where I lay.

"As you know, we use the magic around us as well as the force within ourselves. Some people have a lot, some only a little, for most it needs to be awoken, that being the intention or not, and very few can never use magic at all even if they have had proper training. Angels have it much more strongly, we are made for it in another way and get far more power, but the principle is the same. Different colours answer to different people, and the varying types of magic has varying strengths and uses." I nodded. I could follow him that far. I myself was best at blue magic.

"Djinns are another matter," the magician continued to explain, "their magic is of another kind, and they carry it inside them. This is why too much can literally make them burst at the seams. Maybe you could help them handle it, or take the pressure off in some way. If you get an idea, please tell me if you need any help at all." Alexis well knew how handy my crazy imagination could be.

I nodded again and took another deep drink of my chocolate. "When do you think I will be able to walk again?" I asked him.

Alexis shrugged, "It shouldn't be long. The pain is passing and you should recover your power as well. Are your own supplies of magic through?"

I shook my head, "You used far more force than I did. I do not have enough for larger projects, but it is enough to balance the magic from outside of me. It should be fine."

"Well, then it is simply a matter of…" Alexis started but was interrupted by the doorbell. He rose to go and open the door while muttering, "Since when is this Paddington station?"

"No peace nor quiet in this corridor any longer, right Alex?" I teased him.

I heard upset voices from outside and could eventually identify my brother. I rose, steadier than I had expected, and walked towards the closed door to the atria. As I got closer, I could make out their words.

"...is my sister, and in case it escaped your notice, your best friend. And she almost got killed yesterday. YOU almost got her killed. But you are not at all interested in where she is?"

"Sure, I am," Alexis replied calmly. "But, as ever, you're the one who lost her, not me. If I was to look every time you didn't know where she was, every time you, aware or not, lost your sister, I would be stuck doing nothing else, *ever*."

I could hear my brother run out of patience, and opened the door to the atria. I closed it behind me before I went towards them. My brother stood with his foot in the door, preventing Alexis from shutting it. Not that Alexis seemed to have any such plans. He mostly looked amused. "Stop teasing Thomas," I ordered Alexis. The angel had already reached out a hand to support me. Thomas was obviously not the only one who worried about me, even if Alex was slightly better informed.

"You just can't *not* do that, can you?" Thomas burst out in a tone which was mixing anger and exasperation, but also had a hint implying he was slightly amused.

"Nope," answered Alexis simply and lifted one hand. With a simple spell, obviously, he made the air curl and my brother was instantly tossed against the opposite wall in the hallway outside. I was just about to enlighten Alexis as to just a few of the reasons why he acted like an idiot, when I realised that I could just as well simply leave it. Sometimes, the male world is just as elaborately weird as the magical or academic one, and this was clearly beyond me. Because my brother, who was lying in a small heap next to the wall, was starting to laugh, almost giggle, and three seconds later he was laughing helplessly. Alexis, leaning on the door, did the same thing. Sometimes, things are just entirely un-understandable. I went past my magical brother into my own annex and closed

the door. And here, I had always assumed I was the strange
sibling. Eh, not so much.

Chapter 9

"Why?" everyone looked up, expressing different levels of surprise. Everyone except a couple of djinns and Alexis, neither seemingly very moved by the sudden outburst. We were sitting in one of the older conference rooms, discussing research grants. It still shocked me to realise that I was expected to be present at meetings like that, but then I had only been the academic 'first lady' for three days. Officially.

The professor responsible since over forty years for the classes in above ground level magical defence waved her hands in frustration and elaborated, "Why did they attack us at that very moment? Why not pick a moment when master Darn was not in the hall, or await the not only end, but oblivion of the first attack?" Several of her colleagues agreed.

"Simple," Alexis answered, not looking up from his notes. "I had been yet more dangerous outside, I could have led the djinns from there. That happened anyway, but they were badly informed on the magical prowess of some, so they did not count on that." It was obvious to me that he spoke of Charl, but he said no name and no one else seemed to make the connection. And how could they have?

"Irria imagined that she could take me, and wanted to face me head on," Alexis continued, "and as far as timing is concerned the djinns had a hunch, I'd say, that I did not drop my inquiries into the situation with the healers, which was completely accurate. I suspected Irria, despite her private little speech for my benefit on human rights, and she knew that. She wanted to act before I had gotten prepared and, as far as she knew, gotten invincible. Turns out that to her, at least, I was anyway, but she obviously didn't know that. She counted on me growing complacent as I've been unthreatened for so long. And they chose dinner simply to exclude the djinns from the battle." Like so many times after a statement by Alex, complete silence was reigning. I couldn't help a small smile.

Later that day, I dropped a very heavy book onto my own toes. I could never remember afterwards if I found what I was searching for because I dropped the book, as in it opened up on the right page or something, or if I actually dropped it because I *had* found something, but I'll live with it.

Just after Kiera's 19th Birthday
(About one and a half years later)

With a smile, I shooed my enormous, but still only half grown, Bernersenner named Collie from my—now rather hairy—carpet and pronounced a sweeping spell. My desk, which quite coincidentally was crowded under amulets I'd made, feathers and various tools, was today even more messy than normal. On an otherwise well-kept part of the desk, two amulets were placed. One of them was made in silver, engraved in blue and purple, and the other was a simple oak amulet, still glowing vaguely with blue and red magic.

A light skimmer of yellow magic shone over a simple leather collar Alexis and I had designed for Collie earlier in the day, and the entire desktop was shimmering with my blue magic. The amulets I had spent months designing were soon ready to be used. The one I had given an outer shell of oak was not quite finished, but the magic it needed now wasn't a kind which I could wield. Dhrar had helped me with the silver one, on and off, without realising what I was doing, but without asking, either. Now it was Alexis help that I needed.

I focused on Collie while I waited for Alex to finish his own experiments for the day and turn up. He had promised to drop by around one o'clock, and it was currently a quarter to one, so I did not need to wait for long. "What is it you need a hand with?" Alexis wondered as he showed up, exactly on time. I picked up the oak medallion from my worktable and explained what I wanted him to do for me before I handed it over to him.

Alexis nodded in understanding at my explanation, but when he accepted the magical jewellery, his face expressed a surprise I could not recall seeing with him before. He still did as I had asked, and held it out for me to take it back. I shook my head with a small smile and said, "Around your neck." As soon as the chain touched the skin there, the air started to glitter, and Alex fell onto his knees with a muffled scream. I helped him get to his own workshop and left him on the daybed, studying my jewellery craftsmanship with a small smile. He did not take the chain off his neck.

I found Charl in the library, surrounded by dusty old books and deeply riveted by an ancient djinn tome. Sometimes hir was so obviously not a djinn teenager that it was frankly ridiculous. The ancient djinn looked up and gave me a smile as I appeared behind hir. "Hi, little magician!" hir greeted me.

"Hi Charl," I answered quietly.

Through an Angel's Eyes

Alexis Darn went past the part of the university where they taught the children who were already about to study magic, as he pondered things. He often thought of Kiera as he passed this part of the ancient buildings. It frequently surprised him how much of this place he could connect to her, when he had lived here without her for quite literally a thousand years.

Kiera had never come here. They were all children of magicians, academics or scientists, in many cases all three, most of them raised on the university grounds, and Kiera had not even had her magic awoken when she arrived. Not to mention the unknown fact that she had not even been able to write her own name before he had taught her how to. Thomas was an academic, straight through, but their parents had truly not been.

They were never many children here, but there were always some. The beginners, due to awaken their magic, were usually between nine and eleven years old. Alexis paused outside the open doorway of their classroom and leaned against the wall, meanwhile twisting the air just a little to prevent him from being noticed.

One of the basic mages, Alexis' sharp angel's memory tentatively supplied the name Errol, attempted to explain some basic principle to his students. The grand magician's smile faltered as he watched it play out. The young man had taken one of the older truths about magic to heart; fear raised the probability of reaching into your magic reserves and powers. While this was certainly true enough, Alexis felt his own magic tremble with anger when he saw how this man used it.

Errol attacked the students wickedly, by the look of it scaring them quite a bit, to try and provoke a response. Alexis, who had seen this technique before, and far more often than he would have liked to, knew that it could be not only effective, but dangerous as well, never mind the more important fact that it treated children in a way that no one should. If you wanted to do more than to just summon magic, too, teach and help the child into becoming a controlled, safe magician, calm was by far the superior technique.

Alexis stepped out of his illusion and entered the classroom without knocking. He lifted Errol with magic and threw him into a wall without preamble. He then proceeded to attack him systematically, leaving him no chance at even attempting to mount a defence, while he calmly explained to him that he ought to take his lesson seriously and stop shouting. "What are you doing?" howled the younger man finally.

"The same thing you did to your students," Alexis answered politely. "Attacking you to teach you how to defend yourself. And… as you might have discovered, setting you up against an impossible task."

"That is a completely different matter!" Errol growled.

"Not at all, it is the same impossible resistance, quite fair," the storm-master answered coolly.

Before the angel met Kiera, he would probably have left the classroom at that point, raging in silence. Now he turned towards the students, and explained kindly, "If you wish to

Wake your magic, and intend to learn how to control it, you should find a quiet place, and try to *feel* it. Inside yourselves, and *outside*, too. Try to find it within yourselves, so that you can grasp and control it!" and with a kind smile, the magician left.

Alexis gathered the headmaster's attention during dinner. "I would like to take over the teaching of the first magic class for children," he announced neutrally. I thought that the jaws of the academics and teachers would, quite literally, hit the floor. The noise level in the rest of the hall didn't change, but up by the head tables, it had gone silent.

"What…? Why?" the headmaster actually stuttered in his surprise. Alexis shrugged. "Why not. I do not currently teach, and now when my pupil has surpassed me, I am hardly needed as a craft magician either."

"Surpassed?" somebody naturally wondered, but they got no reply. "I think that Errol does wrong in how he treats young students, and thus I want to take over from him," Alex made clear. "Either you let me do so, or you let us fight it out ourselves," he finished.

"If you'd like to teach, you can take the grand master class in…" one of the scientists suggested hopefully. Alexis shook his head.

"That I am not interested in." Errol, who wasn't qualified to sit at either head table yet, came over to our part of the hall to defend himself.

The headmaster listened for a couple of minutes before shaking his head. "Since grand master Darn is more qualified," a number of coughs and clearings of throats were heard, "I will hand the post over to him," he announced.

I had fallen asleep in front of my computer, watching a film, a very rare occupation for me, when Collie's bark awoke me and at the same time announced that I had a visitor. Three seconds later, there was a knock on the outer door, steps and then the door to the atria was opened. Alexis entered, with an unusually honest smile.

"It isn't even ten o'clock yet," he informed me and sat down next to me. "Exactly how tired do you get in the evenings? I keep telling you, it isn't natural to rise as early as your brother would have you do!" he teased. I sighed and sat up on the thick carpet.

"For your information, I rarely rise before eight o'clock anymore, smartass," I told him and stretched. "So how has your day been? Except shocking everybody at dinner?"

Alexis was holding up a feather. It was a dark purple, but of a quality which made me suspect what it was. The magician handed me the feather. "Did you use K'siri-genes to make the amulet you gave me?" he wondered curiously.

"It is one of yours?" I exclaimed incredulously. "I thought they would turn dark blue or black!"

Alex laughed, "That'd be impossible to predict. It's of no matter. Seriously." He was silent for a short while. "It has only been hours, so this is the only effect I have felt, but I can tell. Since I cut my wings away, the feathers have been growing slowly, and... lost, but this isn't the case now. You can see this one. It is several inches long, six hours later. Angels have a fantastic ability to heal and regrow limbs after injuries, and whatever is actually happening, you awoke it."

"Do you think that it will work?" I wondered.

Alex shrugged, "I don't know. I hope so. But in any case, you've gotten very far. Not even I can change an angel's physiology, but you have proved now that you can. We can always keep trying." The curtailed angel looked at me, "Right?"

I gave him a light nudge to the side, "Of course."

"It is possible to change an angel's physiology," he stated, half lost in thought, "I never thought I'd see that day."

"Oh no," I replied with a teasing smile, "but you shouldn't care for the *rules* so much!"

Alex smiled, obligingly scratching Collie's neck. I watched them silently for a few moments. "I made another amulet, too," I then admitted. Alexis gaze rested on me searchingly, but he didn't speak. Maybe he didn't need to. "For Charl. Dhrar helped me with the djinn magic," I continued, "I gave it to Charl just before noon today. Hir said hir could feel it. Hir thought that it helped. We can just wait and see."

"I hope that it will," was the silent, eyes downcast statement of the angel magician.

Chapter 10

"Where did this come from?" my brother lifted the purple feather, which had hidden itself in my carpet, and brought it up into the light.

Dhrar looked at him with a frown, "That's an angel's feather," he stated in surprise.

"Oh, I have been looking for that!" I admitted and reached a hand out for it.

"You could have asked for a new one!" Alex, who had appeared in the doorway, offered. The angel was still wearing jeans, like many angels did, but had traded his dark blue shirt to a classic, loosely tailored angel's shirt.

The reason for this was obvious as he approached. In the openings of the fabric there were glimpses of purple. "I would pull out more feathers for you, Kiera, but it hurts!" Alexis continued with obvious delight.

"Turn!" I exclaimed, almost unable to avoid peeking through my fingers. It had been three days since I had given him the pendant. But even with the amazing recuperative powers of angels, could something have happened yet? Then again, the feathers had started to change their colour after three *hours*.

Alexis, laughing, turned around for me. His wings had regrown. They were barely a metre from the tip of one wing to the other, which was normal for angel children after the age of seven, but they had regrown. And I assumed they hadn't stopped growing yet. "Come!" I asked. I sat up on my window table, as the desk was outright perilous to sit on, and Alexis came to kneel before it, his back against me. "Are they hurting?" I asked and gently followed the shape of his wing with my hand, feeling the smooth, soft feathers.

"Not at all, if I do not try to unfold them," I could hear the grin in his voice. "But then again, I do do that. I have full feeling in them, and mobility, as long as I am careful," he turned partly around to look at me, "I can hardly wait until I can unfold and let them carry me, but I realise that will be some time yet. And honestly speaking, after all these years…"

"You can wait just a little bit more," I smiled in reply.

Only then, I noticed how Dhrar and Thomas stood and stared at us with their mouths open, in any case Thomas did. The latter was obviously trying to form a sentence, but he didn't do very well. Not a sound came out. Dhrar managed, after a moment, somewhat better. "This was what you needed my help with?" hir questioned. I shook my head.

"No, this one I managed myself, except a smaller charm by Alexis towards the end. It was a djinn-charm I needed djinn magic for."

"And a masterly performed such," Alex, now stood up again, cut in.

"Is it working?" I asked.

"Perfectly," the answer came from Charl, who had entered the room silently, unnoticed until speaking. And hir had probably not even been sneaking on purpose.

Timing such as that was only possible in the world of film, and of magic, where magicians got in touch in the most unexpected ways. The djinn closed the little pendant Alexis had used to summon his very old friend to join us, and smiled at me. "I can never thank you enough, young human girl," the magical being assured, for the first time actually sounding like the other truly old djinns I had had occasion to meet, once or twice. Hir usual confusion was gone without a trace. "For the first time I can fully control my own power," the djinn explained and hir voice was fervent, "it is a gift I can never repay." The djinn bowed to me and then gave Alexis a warm smile. "You seem to be equally indebted to your young apprentice."

The angel nodded, "Always."

Charl smiled, "I have notified a very shocked administration that I am the djinn whom they read about in legend, and with your permission I would be very happy to help you in your new teaching endeavour.

"The academics find it a waste, of course, but I have found that the most important resource we have is young minds."

"That makes two of us. Again," Alexis answered laughing. I had never seen him quite like this before. The two magicians embraced. "Can you take the class tomorrow? I need to stay away and care for my wings, as they grow."

"Of course," answered Charl, with a light, very djinnish bow of just his head.

Dhrar, who had realised just who hir stood before, was silent, hir head turned away, but Thomas, who wasn't a djinn and who, different from me, never did study angels, dared to ask, "How big does the wings of an adult angel grow?"

"Two metres per wing," I answered in a low voice, "so they should grow about four times larger." I turned back to Alex and gave him a stern look, "And you aren't allowed to fly yet for three weeks!"

Midsummer's Eve
(Same Year)

I walked up to the shelf next to my bed and studied the exquisite silver diadems which laid there. I had only known Alexis for about a month or two when he gave me the first one, decorated with blue pearls. The second was from my most djinn-inspired period, and looked thus. The third was strewn with different blue flowers, complete with green stalks and green grass. The fourth, suitable for the diameter of my fully grown head, was decorated with lively forget-me-nots, my favourite flower.

This one, I took down, and carefully placed in my hair, braiding the naked threads at the back into the pulled back furthermost locks of my hair, achieving a slightly fairylike feeling I've always found perfect for midsummer's eve. I blame Shakespeare. My dress, green with black at the hem and lacing, was open in the back, a fact almost entirely hidden by my free-flowing hair.

Alexis and Charl, nowadays always found most everywhere in each other's company, were waiting for me in the Dark Corridor. The angel, announcing that he certainly was secure enough in his masculinity to have deep purple wings and thus refusing to even hear of bleaching them white, naturally did no longer wear his magician's cape. He, as well as the djinn, wore magnificent cloaks, Alexis' in black (he rarely wore blue anymore since his wings grew out) and Charl's in green. Both congratulated me on my very diplomatic colour choices.

"Will you both be able to perform the spell I asked for?" I asked as we started to walk together. The djinn merely nodded, but Alex, after having made clear that it was doable, although hard, and would be fine in the end, specified by quoting Getafix in the usual order. "I need lots of what I'm needing!"

"You never did tell me who the last one is," I realised as we went around a corner, "you've always said you have three favourite book characters. You obviously keep Skalman," I winked at Charl, "in the highest honour, and you barely go a day without quoting Getafix, but who is the third?"

"Tiger Lily!" the djinn revealed teasingly.

"Well, yes…" Alexis said vaguely, "she always has a simple solution. Let's go that way, kill that bad guy and the problem is solved. Life would so much simpler if that was actually true!"

"Life might be easier, but not better, if that was how it worked," Charl pointed out. "I always preferred Barrie for his humour myself, not his sense of justice!"

"Well, there is that too!" the magician answered with a nod. "But you make it sound like the red something in *Alice in Wonderland*, 'off with his head!' That is not what it's about." His voice was chiding as he objected.

"We know," I stated, smiling. "I like that there's three of them, completing and helping each other to achieve something great!"

"Yes, that's nice," the djinn answered with a mysterious smile. "And that definitely makes you the hero of that collection."

"I agree. We all know who you'd be... weird magical being doing apparent nonsense no one gets," Alexis teased Charl, who retorted, "'Curious-er and curious-er,' said Alice," with a smile. I broke down.

Charl leaned in closer while we passed the huge windows of the entrance hall and the angel watched the sky outside. "Thank you," the djinn whispered. "Did you know, that they built the annex and the Dark Corridor specifically for Alexis during the twelfth century or hundreds? I wasn't here then— I had troubles of my own, as you know—but he lived here, and he so much desired to be alone, that he got his own, lonely, part of the buildings to live in.

"It comes down entirely to you that he finally came of out that diamond hard shell he lived in for so long. Even all the other things I so have to thank you for aside, thank you so much!"

"One for all, all for one!" I answered, smiling. Alex absent-mindedly turned back to us from the sky as we passed the windows, away from the blue midsummer's sky, and all three of us walked through the hallway to open up the closed oak doors into the great hall, where I knew all the rest of my friends, and the rest of my family, were waiting for me.

Other Books by L. H. Westerlund

In Your Pants – A Brief History in Nerdfighteria
The Truth About Monsters – The Pixie and the Monster
Underneath the Bed

L. H. Westerlund's next novel will be published this summer!